The TEMPTATION
and DOWNFALL
of the VICAR
# of STANTON LACY

Peter Klein

D1428703

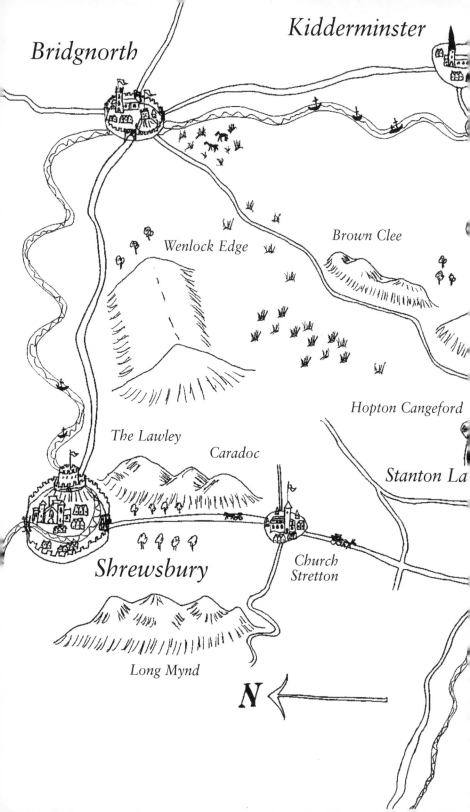

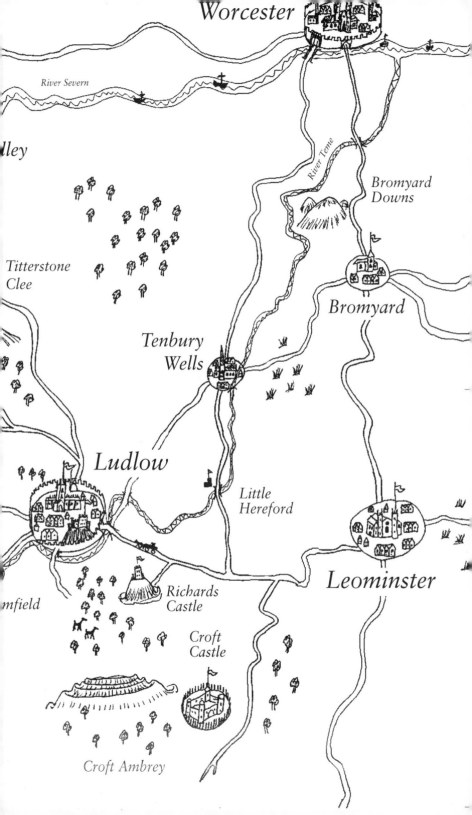

First published in Great Britain by Merlin Unwin Books, 2005
Revised, updated and redesigned in larger print in 2015
Reprinted 2020

Copyright © Peter Klein, 2005

All rights reserved, including the right to reproduce this book
or portions thereof in any form or by any means, electronic or
mechanical, including photocopying, recording, or by any
information storage and retrieval system, without permission
in writing from the publisher. All inquiries should be addressed
to the publisher:

Merlin Unwin Books
Palmers House
7 Corve Street
Ludlow
Shropshire SY8 1DB
U.K.

The author asserts his moral right to be identified with this work.

Designed and set in Sabon by Merlin Unwin

Printed by Short Run Press, Devon, England

ISBN 978-1-873674-71-0

The TEMPTATION and DOWNFALL of the VICAR of STANTON LACY

Being the Story of Robert Foulkes,
the Late Vicar of the
Parish of Stanton Lacy near Ludlow, in Shropshire
who was Tried, Convicted, and Sentenced for Murder
at the Sessions House in the Old Bailey, London
on January 16th 1679,
and Executed on the 31st following.

MERLIN UNWIN BOOKS

'You may in me see... what it is for one who was a Member of Christ, to make himself the Member of a Harlot.'

Robert Foulkes
Tyburn, 31st January 1679

Front cover: *An Alarme for Sinners* pamphlet, 1679 original supplied by the author, costumes kindly provided by Amy Ormond and Moreton Hall, and with special thanks to Elfrid Unwin.

CONTENTS

Opposite: Stanton Lacy parish church and churchyard as it looked about 100 years ago. From a photograph taken by W.A.Call of Monmouth.

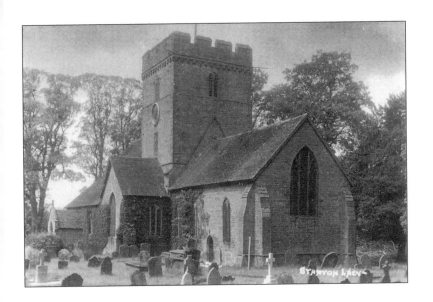

PREFACE

The Beginnings of a Mystery

In the autumn of 1968, a man from Ludlow travelled a couple of miles north to visit St. Peter's church at Stanton Lacy. His purpose was to take some photographs of this important Saxon church for a historian friend. But when he got there, he was overcome by an 'eerie feeling of terror' when standing in the chancel, and he left without his photographs. Later he returned with his wife, but again came the inexplicable feeling of fear, so the couple decided to contact the vicar, the Reverend Prebendary L J Blashford Snell. He accompanied the man into the church, witnessing his hair apparently standing on end, and this extraordinary incident was even reported in local and national newspapers[1].

The vicar later mentioned a local story about the murder of a young man by Cromwellian troops in or near the church during the Civil War; and crudely carved into the chancel arch there is an inscription, possibly commemorating this death in

1649. Someone had recorded it in 1952, so perhaps it was to this that Prebendary Snell referred. Whatever the explanation, the story demonstrates that the small and apparently quiet village of Stanton Lacy may harbour secrets and stories of which few people are aware.

I ought, however, to add here that I have spent many happy and serene hours in Stanton Lacy church without the slightest misgivings, or any experiences other than feelings of profound peace, and an awareness of the passing of history. For most the church is a supremely tranquil place, and this is attested by the many messages of appreciation in its visitor's book. It was, however, in the mid-1970s, before researching the history of the church and while writing the first edition of the present guide, that I first encountered Robert Foulkes. The printed edition of the parish register, published in 1903, rather baldly lists him as follows:

> 1660-78 Robert Foulkes, inducted 12 Sep., 1660;
> executed 31 Jan., 1678-9[2]

The book briefly goes on to say: *The Rev. Robert Foulkes, Vicar 1660-1678, was the chief actor in a notorious tragedy, to which, strangely enough, there is not the slightest allusion in the Registers.* Three pamphlets were published at the time of Foulkes' death, one of which was written by Foulkes himself while awaiting execution. This features and is quoted in John Fowles' novel *The Magus*, and even Foulkes himself puts in a brief appearance. Apart from this, the story is little known, and much of the detail has remained obscure. It deserves better. This book draws together the complicated threads of this story for the first time. There is no happy ending, but it does bring to light a fascinating tale of humanity.

Peter Klein
Pembridge, 2005

Opposite: A 17th-century woodblock illustration from a ballad sheet, showing a hanging of the period. It shows well the excitement of the occasion, with the press of the throng gathered around the gallows, and the ring of pikemen to stand guard and control the crowd.

CHAPTER 1

The Three-Legged Mare

It was a freezing morning on the last Friday in January, 1679. Shortly after ten o'clock, a subdued figure in black was escorted out of the press-yard of the grim and pestilential London prison known as Newgate. Being a clergyman, he was allowed the privilege of the Ordinary's coach rather than the usual cart; and with him were the several grave and eminent churchmen who were to accompany their passenger on this last brief journey of his life – a matter of a mere two and a half miles.

As the great bell of St. Sepulchre's church tolled, the coach lurched slowly away, preceded by a hearse, and flanked by an escort of constables with staves, and pikemen. As it passed the church steps, the cortège paused for the customary address by the bellman of St. Sepulchre's, and a cup of wine and a nosegay were offered in at the coach window. Then it rattled

1

over the cobbles down Snow Hill, over Holborn Bridge and the Fleet River, up to High Holborn and through St. Giles's, and out onto the highroad leading towards Oxford.

As for our passenger, a former minister from a far-away rural parish in Shropshire, he now had little inclination to observe the excitement and flurry of work-a-day activities in the streets as he passed by. He and his companions were too earnestly absorbed in prayer, in rapt preparation for the final and terrible scene of his life. In the wake of the coach, an excitable throng was already following, swelling in size as the cavalcade passed on its way. At the church of St. Giles-in-the-Fields a bowl of ale was offered to him as his last refreshment – a small gesture of kindness in an unforgiving world. After no more than half an hour his destination was now in sight – a robust utilitarian structure of massive wooden beams, triangular in plan and some eighteen feet high, erected at the junction of three roads, and close to what is today Marble Arch. This was the infamous hanging-tree, the Deadly Nevergreen, the Three-Legged Mare of Tyburn.

Here, encircled by a ghoulish crowd, was played out the grisly conclusion to events that took place over three hundred years ago, and much of that story will be told here in the words of those who were directly involved. And yet, despite its remoteness from us in time, it is in many ways as familiar a tale of human passion, weakness, and folly, as any told in headlines splashed across the front pages of our more lurid tabloids today. It is the tale of a man who should have been the steady, dependable rock at the core of his Christian community but who, in his own words, yielded to 'an unclean, a filthy devil' within him. There had followed an Old Bailey trial, sentence, and this very public humiliation and retribution. He was condemned to dance what the gleeful watching multitude had gruesomely dubbed, the 'Tyburn jig'.

At the time it was a national scandal, especially for the Church, because in Stuart England the Church was an integral part of the State's apparatus of government. What we would regard today as fundamentalist Protestantism was then the national religion, and those who were unwilling to conform to it were regarded at very least with suspicion. Those who refused to acknowledge its authority, and thus the prerogative of the King at its head, could be deemed a subversive threat to State security. Individuals, whether catholics, non-conformists, or simply the irreligious, were fined or harassed. Some were threatened with barbaric torments, if not brutally punished, even on occasion for completely imaginary offences. Indeed Foulkes' execution took place at the height of the mass hysteria generated by 'The Popish Plot', when Titus Oates, aided and abetted by Parliament, fabricated an imagined Catholic conspiracy to assassinate Charles the Second. While the Plot does not impinge directly upon our story, it does reflect the fears and powerful forces at loose in a society dominated by religion. The parish was the instrument of local government and social control, and Charles the First had once declared England to be 'ruled from the pulpit.' Attendance in church once a week and partaking of Communion were compulsory, and most male members of the parish were expected to attend their vestry, and were annually elected to serve terms as local officials, such as churchwardens and Overseers of the Poor. The role of parish priest was therefore an onerous one, for he was presumed to be a man of stature, beyond reproach, and a Christian example to all. If he failed to live up to these expectations, then the integrity and authority of the system came under threat.

To add to the compulsory religious observance, and the expected conformity to acceptable Christian behaviour, within the parish community there were eyes and ears that were ever alert to detect departure from what was expected. Churchwardens were duty-bound to act upon information, and a liability to be presented might be particularly apparent where an individual had made enemies. In rural communities especially, this suspicion of dissent or deviance was common, although in the more densely packed towns it tended to break down, and immorality and crime were rife.

While these historical circumstances are very much of their time, the essential story of Robert Foulkes is timeless, and all too familiar to us, and as we read we can easily forget the passing of the years, and view it almost as a contemporary

Above: The village of Stanton Lacy, and its Saxon parish church, are today almost entirely shrouded in trees, as this view from the north-west shows. Rising behind, and bathed in autumn sunshine, is the Hope; and beyond that is Whitbatch.

event. If the study of history shows us anything, it is that our human frailties are still much as they have always been; only the backdrop is different. No account of Foulkes' life, therefore, would be complete unless some mention was made of the landscape, people, and times that helped to shape him. So first we need to set him against the background of the parish where he lived and worked, for most of the parishioners that Foulkes encountered were Shropshire born and bred, with roots that went back in this border landscape for hundreds if not thousands of years.

Overleaf: The fertile valley floor of the river Corve provided the wealth that, during the mid-11th century, built the fine late Saxon church at Stanton Lacy. In the foreground of this view is The Barn farm. Beyond it to the east lies the village; and beyond that is the high ground of Titterhill and Hayton's Bent.

CHAPTER 2

Stanton Lacy

The parish of Stanton Lacy has at its centre the finest surviving
Saxon church in Shropshire, dedicated to St. Peter, much of
which dates from shortly before the Norman Conquest;
and there are also signs of what may have been a circular
churchyard. Whether this implies the existence of a former
prehistoric enclosure, or alternatively an earlier Christian site,
is as yet unexplored.

This feature is however not the only visible sign of
antiquity, and the roots of this community go back far further,
as a glance about the surrounding landscape plainly shows.
Surrounded by hills, and drained by the rivers Corve, Onny
and Teme, recent archaeology has shown that this flat fertile
valley floor was being cleared for agriculture some 5500 years

ago, during the early Neolithic period. There is good evidence that occupation increased in intensity into the Bronze Age, supporting thriving family communities somewhere near-by. Within a mile of the church to the south-west, on the far side of the river Corve, are the remains of a barrow field, a large group of Bronze Age burial mounds, of which there were originally about twenty in number, together with a large cremation cemetery which remained in use for a thousand years. This area, known as the Old Field, continued as the site of pagan burials and cemeteries on through into the early Anglo Saxon period. In Foulkes' day there was an alehouse and bowling green there; but today it is better known simply as the site of Ludlow Race Course, and the Golf Club.

In Roman times a villa or farmstead stood about 500 yards to the north of St. Peter's parish church, slight remains of which were found during field drainage in 1910. Intensive farming continued throughout the Saxon period until, by the time of the Domesday Book in 1086, Stantun as it was now called, the place of the stones, or perhaps on stony ground, was at the centre of some of the richest and most productive land in Shropshire, amply shown by the number of plough-teams, and its population. This provided the wealth that by about 1050 had helped to build a large stone cruciform church, much of which survives today in the north and west walls of the nave, and the north transept. According to the Domesday Book, at the Conquest Stanton had been held by a Saxon freeman named Siward. He was probably the 'rich man of Shropshire', Siward son of Ethelgar, who, according to the monk chronicler Orderic Vitalis, was in the service of the great Norman Marcher lord Roger de Montgomery. Siward had also been involved in the founding of another church dedicated to St. Peter outside the east gate at Shrewsbury, later to become the Benedictine abbey site.

7

Stanton Lacy parish church is therefore among the oldest in the country, and over the succeeding centuries was further altered and enlarged, being given a chancel almost as long as the nave during the 13th-century. A new south aisle was added during the early 14th-century; and the powerful Mortimer family built a sturdy bell-tower and south transept in about 1330. Despite a sweeping Victorian 'restoration' in 1847, including new windows and the clearance of its interior, Stanton church remains today much as it was during Robert Foulkes' day, and he would have little difficulty in recognizing it.

In Foulkes' time, the parish was a sizeable one of some 7000 acres, then including what later became the parish of Hopton Cangeford, and it had a population of over 400[3]. It was and still is divided into two portions, its boundaries perhaps representing at least in part the bounds of the Saxon manor of Stanton. Between these two portions lies part of the parish of Bromfield, and during the late 11th-century the parish and town of Ludlow was created out of its south-western extremity, on the banks of the river Teme, and less than three miles away across the fields.

Here, on an excellent natural defensive site on a hilltop, Ludlow's great tower keep and castle were built by the Norman Marcher lords. The town was encircled by a substantial defensive wall and ditch; and the castle was further developed and elaborated by the Mortimers, and under the Tudors became the seat of the Princes of Wales.

Between 1534 and 1641 it was also the headquarters of the Court of the Council in the Marches of Wales, the regional centre of government for the whole of the principality. Here what has been aptly called a 'bureaucratic anthill' of judges, lawyers, clerks, and administrators, implemented the edicts and instructions from Westminster and the Royal Court in London.

It therefore comes as little surprise that Ludlow was a Royalist stronghold at the time of the Civil War. In 1646, after a punishing siege lasting six weeks, during which many buildings had been burned or damaged, if not already pulled down to clear the town wall for defence, Ludlow finally opened its gates to Parliament, and a period of prolonged stagnation followed. As the result of an Act of Parliament that had abolished the Court in 1641, Ludlow had been deprived of an important part of its livelihood in supplying the castle with provisions, stationery, building materials, labour, and all

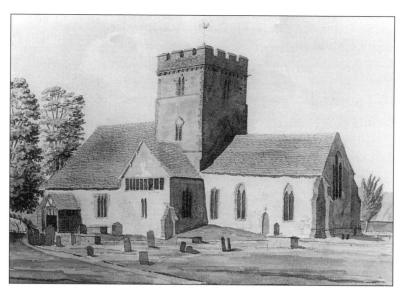

Watercolour view of Stanton Lacy parish church, drawn in 1790 by the Rev. Edward Williams, a Shropshire antiquary. Elm trees then surrounded the churchyard, and this sketch shows the church very much as Foulkes would have known it. High up in the south wall of the south transept can be seen a long rectangular window, that threw light onto the crossing where the Communion table would have been placed. This window was replaced in 1849 during the Victorian 'restoration'. (*Shropshire Archives*).

the other supplies needed by a busy government department. During the Commonwealth Ludlow became a depressed garrison town, controlled from Shrewsbury by the County Committee. The grand houses of the lawyers now had other occupants or stood empty, and the inns no longer catered for the flurry of comings and goings of the visitors who had flocked to the castle for justice. Even the great parish church was stripped of its 15th-century organ, as the dreary hand of Puritanism took its hold.

With the Restoration of Charles the Second in 1660, life had slowly begun to return once again; and Robert Foulkes, who had arrived in Ludlow some three years before, will have witnessed the gradual revival of the town's fortunes as the Court was re-established, although after his death it was to survive for barely a further decade. Though distant from the national centre of government, the parishioners of Stanton Lacy were thereby better placed than many to make direct contact with people of influence, and had lines of communication open to them that others would have found much more difficult to access. Here too, in the St. John's Chapel of Ludlow parish church, was held the consistory court of the Bishop of Hereford, then presided over by his Commissioner Sir Timothy Baldwyn, where the bishop's authority was enforced, and where matters of lay and clerical parochial discipline were heard. Among this court's main functions were the proving of wills, the enforcement of church attendance and payment of parochial dues or fines, the detection and fining of recusants or catholic dissenters, and the punishment of lapses in morality. Here, too, parishioner could sue parishioner, in a litigious age when lawyers were at their most abundant. It is the record books and other surviving papers of this court, now housed in the Herefordshire Record Office, that have provided much of the material for this story.

CHAPTER 3

Foulkes' Predecessors

'Mr Clayton calls himself a doctor, yet he is a man of that behaviour, that I have seldom known his fellow, and if credit be given to his oath, every man that he beareth malice unto will be utterly undone.'

During the 17th-century the clergy were, as at any time, unique individuals of varying strengths and character. To put Robert Foulkes in perspective, therefore, it is certainly worthwhile comparing him with those that preceded him in office, if only to get some idea of the variety of men that a relatively remote parish such as this might attract. The vicars were increasingly university graduates; and they were almost invariably outsiders, although they were not alone in this. By the 17th-century the

11

population was far from static, and it becomes clear during the later legal proceedings, as we shall see, that a number of Foulkes' more influential parishioners, of yeoman stock, were from elsewhere in the county, moving from tenancy to tenancy. Some had only been in Stanton Lacy a matter of months, and one indeed arrived only six weeks before the events to be described took place.

In 1634 John Whateley had passed away, having been vicar at Stanton Lacy since the reign of Queen Elizabeth, after an incumbency of 47 years. He was a man who, according to the parish register, had 'lived religiously, preached painfully, and died comfortably' there on the first of July. We know little else of him except that he had been ordained by the Bishop of Gloucester, and that he was well educated, perhaps at grammar school or university, but had no degree. He made a will just a month before he died, and amongst other bequests he left his son, William, fifty pounds in cash, together with the rest of his books that remained and were 'not yet sent to him in London'.[4] A total of forty shillings he left to the parish poor, who were to be divided into three groups of ten, chosen by his widow according to their need. Here, apparently, we have a vision of a thoroughly decent and well-respected man, who died peacefully and full of years among his own community.

Onto this scene of apparent bucolic tranquillity arrived 'Dr' Ralph Clayton, possibly the Yorkshireman of that name who had matriculated from Lincoln College, Oxford, in 1605 at the age of 16. By September 1634, he now claimed to be a 'Doctor of Sacred Theology', but where this degree was obtained is a complete mystery, as there is no record of him having continued at any university; and there appears to have been some doubt even at the time. Yorkshire, particularly the West Riding, and the area around Hull, was renowned as a stronghold of puritanism, but whether this might have had any bearing on Clayton's bizarre behaviour is open to speculation. Whatever, in July 1637 Sir John Bridgeman, Chief Justice of Chester and the presiding judge at Ludlow Castle, was writing to Westminster about a man whose activities, to say the least, had raised a few local eyebrows:

'You wish to understand from me the condition of Dr.Clayton. I have perused a presentment upon oath whereby he is accused of, firstly, haunting alehouses, and once continuing in several alehouses in Ludlow from Thursday to Wednesday, neglecting to come to his church, or any other church, on the Sunday. Secondly, for tempting the chastity of divers women; and thirdly, for causing the bells to be rung at the bringing of beer into his house, making those who brought it drunk, and giving the ringers two shillings. I find also information depending against him before the Council in the Marches of Wales, for beating his sexton with a staff in the church on the 7th of March last'.[5]

By March 1638 Clayton's 'condition' had not improved, and we find him imprisoned in Ludlow Castle, with moves clearly afoot to have him ejected from his living. In June legal counsel to Archbishop Laud found Clayton refusing to defend himself on the grounds that his incarceration made it impossible, and he wrote that 'the doctor now lies in prison in Ludlow Castle, he has his liberty of drinking and rioting, and lives as it were in contempt of justice'.[6] In January 1639 Arthur Winwood, chief porter and Clayton's gaoler at the castle, and someone who also just happened to be one of the churchwardens at Stanton Lacy, was summoned to the Star Chamber in London after Clayton had accused him of uttering treasonable remarks. Winwood however carried a letter from Bridgeman's successor, Sir Thomas Milward, that did not mince words:

'Mr Clayton calls himself a doctor, yet he is a man of that behaviour, that I have seldom known his fellow, and if credit be given to his oath, every man that he beareth malice unto will be utterly undone. When I came first to Ludlow he was in the porter's lodge for divers misdemeanours, and this last term he was fined again, and stands committed for the like offences. I beseech you to be informed of Clayton's credit before you give any allowance of his oath.'[7]

Winwood was acquitted within the day, at a hearing held in the presence of the King; and a fortnight later he was granted permission to bring an action against Clayton in the same court.[8] Of Ralph Clayton nothing more is heard, and here he seems to vanish into the dust of history. With benefit of hindsight, that Stanton Lacy should have had to endure two such men as Clayton and Foulkes, within the space of only forty-five years, would seem to suggest that the parish may have been somewhat ill-starred, but the vicar who was Clayton's immediate successor was in contrast quite plainly a man of considerable qualities and stature.

THOMAS ATKINSON, AND CIVIL WAR

'... the most worthy pastor of this church; whose heart was the home of the brightest virtues side by side with knowledge; whose tongue was the polished expounder of a keener judgement; whose hand was the treasure house of the poor ...'

After Clayton's expulsion, greater care was evidently taken in choosing his replacement, and it was Thomas Atkinson, Master of Arts from Trinity College, Oxford, and recently inducted as rector of the wealthy living at nearby Wistanstow, who came to live at Stanton Lacy in May 1639. Patron to both these livings was John Lord Craven of Ryton, who died childless in about 1648, and who was succeeded by his elder brother William Lord Craven, to whom Atkinson became chaplain and possibly a close friend. Atkinson also became related to the Cravens through his second marriage in about 1645. William Craven inherited great wealth, and during his very long life was a career soldier and devoted Royalist supporter, but because of this he had to spend the period of the Commonwealth in exile abroad. As the storm clouds of the Civil War gathered, Atkinson wrote in the parish registers of his feelings about puritanism and the impending wind of change. Under cover of Latin, he wrote: 'Pios multos est rem monstrosam. Scitote posteri, et erubescite', (Much piety is a monstrous thing. Seek to know it, you who succeed us, and blush with shame). This dread of religious fundamentalism seems as pertinent today as it was three and a half centuries ago.

In the summer of 1645, a Parliamentary force swept through the country to the north of Ludlow, and many royalists sought shelter within its walls. It is here that we apparently find Atkinson, or at least his family, when in January 1646 his son John, later a physician and one who figures in this story, was baptized in the parish church. Ludlow surrendered to Parliament in the following June, and for five years we lose track of Atkinson until 1651 when he appears to have returned to Stanton Lacy. The parish register, a number of pages almost blank, comments only upon the lack of entries 'through distractions of the fearfull civill warre and the vicars enforced absence thereupon'. This is then followed by an agonised plea: 'Da pacem domine lassati sumus' (Give us peace, O Lord, for we are wearied).

There is little doubt that during the period of the Civil War the community at Stanton Lacy was probably as riven in its loyalties as most others, for this was a time when even members of families were divided against one another. While most may have remained staunchly loyal to Lord Craven and the King, some will have sympathised with Parliament, or saw that they stood to gain if they collaborated with the winning side. There is little recorded, what with the parish register being suspended during Atkinson's absence, but there is one curious document which, unusually, is in the form of a graffito in the parish church.

On the jamb of the chancel arch on the south side, facing the altar, is a very curious monumental inscription, particularly rare in being cut directly into the church fabric itself. It speaks to us of a tragic event during August 1649, a few months after the trial and execution of Charles the First, and while Cromwell was away suppressing Royalist resistance in Ireland. It is improvised and crudely scratch-carved, abraded and illegible in places, but it commemorates a young man, Richard Heynes of Downton, who died on the 19th August 1649, in his 24th year. Heynes was certainly the local man whose baptism appears in the parish register on the 23rd April 1626. Whoever the writer was, possibly Atkinson himself, he was moved to express himself effusively in Latin, and the words: FLETE NEFAS – Bewail this horrid deed – and: RAPTUS FLORE VIGENTE MEO – Snatched away in the Flower of my Youth – strongly suggest that Heynes was the victim of untimely violence. He ends with a quotation from an ode by Horace: PULVIS ET UMBRA SUMUS – We are but Dust and Shadow – followed by the initials T R , perhaps for TERMINUM RESPICE. The earliest known record of this inscription was taken as recently as 1952; and it may be that a story about someone being pursued and murdered by Parliamentary troops, in or about the church, may have been put forward as an explanation at that time.

With his patron and protector in exile abroad, Atkinson

INOBITV
RICHARD
HEYNES DE
DOWNETON
DORMIENTIS
DIE AVGVSTI
19 1649
ANNO ÆTATIS
SVÆ 24

FLORE VIGEN
TE MEO IACEO
RICHARDVS
HVMATVS

               E N
·RAPTVS FLO
RE VIGENTE
   MEO·
FLETE NEFAS
VESTRVM
CERTVS STAT
TERMINVS
   OMNI·
      ITE MOR
TIALE PVL
VIS ET VM
BRA SVMVS·
 · TR ·

Left: A drawing of the remarkable inscription, scratched into the chancel arch *(above)*, that records the death of Richard Heynes of Downton, who died on the 19th of August, 1649, in his 24th year. Parts are almost illegible, but it reads: 'In the flower of my youth I, Richard, lie buried... Snatched away in the flower of my youth. Bewail this horrid deed. Certain stands the end for all of you. [?] Remember, O Mortal, we are but dust and shadow. T.R.' In parts some letters are very abraded if not later obliterated, while others are still filled with lime wash, and as a result the carving is not easy to photograph.

was now hounded by Parliament probably for merely being so closely associated with Lord Craven, and in June 1651 we find him defending himself before the County Committee for Compounding in Shrewsbury, who had seized his estate, and having to 'beg the heads of the charge of delinquency against him, and leave to examine witnesses'.[9] His persuasive powers may have saved Atkinson, for he succeeded in keeping his vicarage and he appears to have returned to his duties by October 1651, when the entries in the register recommence. Moreover on his memorial inscription, engraved for his widow Elizabeth on a brass plate in the church, and originally placed within the altar rails in the chancel, we read that 'his tongue was the polished expounder of a keener judgement'.[10] He had however been unjustly declared a 'scandalous minister', and deprived of his rectory at Wistanstow for his loyalty to his patron and the Crown.

In his last years, therefore, Atkinson will have lived in somewhat reduced circumstances, and Lord Craven was by then in no position to supplement his basic parochial income. He was however described as Craven's 'chaplaine' in his burial entry in the register, so it seems likely that he had received, during his earlier years at Stanton Lacy, some annual fee or enhancement to his parochial earnings. With his patron in exile abroad and stripped of his estates during the Commonwealth, this almost certainly ceased altogether, as did his income from Wistanstow. Atkinson had the lease of a farm and its farmhouse, which he let out to a tenant, although he and his family occupied much of the house himself. Otherwise, as vicar his income was principally derived from the small or privy tithes; glebe; fees paid at baptisms, marriages, and burials; and also churchings – that is the readmission of women after childbirth. Tithes, in theory a tenth of the annual produce of the parishioners, in Stanton Lacy had long since been commuted to fixed sums of money that, due to inflation, now bore little relation to the actual value of what was produced. Long before the time of Foulkes' incumbency this had included the tithe of hay, normally allocated to the rector or, as here at Stanton Lacy, the 'impropriator'.[11] In fact Atkinson also took the rectoral tithe of corn and grain, but only because he held the right to do so by lease from Lord Craven.[12] We shall see that Foulkes himself was later to be involved in several tithe disputes, although the motive behind bringing these actions is sometimes questionable. Glebe lands were those allocated to a benefice that could either be rented out to tenants, or farmed by the incumbent himself. Lastly, we know from the register that the 'accustomed' fee paid to Foulkes at each marriage was five shillings; and both Atkinson and Foulkes also occasionally recorded 'mortuaries' of ten shillings, a maximum fee paid in lieu of the heriot or tax of the second best chattel taken by the vicar after a death.

Atkinson died on the 8th April 1657, at the age of 53, before happier times returned. He was apparently exhausted, for a correspondent to John Walker, author of *Sufferings of the Clergy*, recorded that he was 'severely or worse handled, which hard usage was believed to have shortened his days'[13]. His will gloomily speaks of every soul 'groaneing under the burden of the earthlie Tabernacle', which latterly may have summed up his opinion of life in general.[14] John Walker also mentioned that a puritan, Major Sanders, succeeded him at Stanton Lacy, but then 'went off at the King's return', although Walker's correspondent, probably mistakenly, gave his name as Major Slaughter.[15] Atkinson left a widow, Elizabeth, who was his third wife, and there were also three children by his second marriage.

His first wife Anne had given him two sons. Both were baptized Thomas and died in infancy and, together with their mother, lay buried at Stanton Lacy by 1643.[16] Then in about 1645 he married an Anne Whitmore of Claverley near Bridgnorth, youngest daughter of John Whitmore of Ludstone Hall, in so doing also marrying into his patron's extended family; and in January 1646 his son John, later a physician, was born and baptized at Ludlow.[17] Next came Francis, born in Stanton Lacy in about 1648, who was to become a parson like his father; and finally there was the daughter Ann, the youngest, born in about 1650. Their mother may have died before Atkinson was reinstated in his parish, possibly immediately after Ann's birth, but there is no record of her burial locally, the registers being suspended until October 1651. She was certainly dead by 1654 because his third wife, Elizabeth, according to her own testimony, first came to Stanton Lacy in about that year. At the age then of about 46 she may have been a widow, although there is never mention of any previous marriage or children. Either way, she acquired a step-daughter Ann, then about four years old, and two step-sons aged eight and six. By 1661 the two boys were up at Christ Church, Oxford, while their sister remained at home.

The already-motherless Ann was but seven years old when her father died, and she was therefore for the most part brought up by her stepmother, Elizabeth. It is however evident, judging from the wording of Thomas Atkinson's will, that the young Ann seems to have been doted upon by her father, and that there may have been a particularly close bond between them. After Elizabeth's death, his will specifically left the lease of the rectoral tithe to Ann. It also expressly desired Elizabeth 'to be carefull of my daughter Ann in A speciall manner, And to add what she pleases towards her porcion'. In addition, Ann was also the beneficiary of the will of her maternal uncle and godfather, William Whitmore, who left her twenty

The engraved brass plate that commemorates Thomas Atkinson in Stanton Lacy parish church. Today the plate is attached to the floor under the tower near the pulpit, but it was originally safely placed within the altar rails, against the east wall of the chancel, until moved in 1849 by the then vicar, Dr. Joseph Bowles. It can be translated:

Sacred unto Eternity
Under this stone await the resurrection of the dead
the most precious remains of Thomas Atkinson, until lately
the most worthy pastor of this church; whose heart was
the home of the brightest virtues side by side with knowledge,
whose tongue was the polished expounder of a keener judgement,
whose hand was the treasure house of the poor, whose daily life
was likewise ordered under the strict rule of Harpocrates [ie. silence].
At length his wearied spirit, as that of a ship much tossed to and fro
by the raging waves of the times, sped forth with the swelled sails
of faith into the haven of the blessed, the bosom of Abraham.
April the 8th A.D. 1657, aged 53 years.
Elizabeth, his beloved wife, grieving, placed (this inscription here)
and consecrated it with her tears.

pounds in 1668.[18] While not a large sum of money, her source of income and her capital were designed to set her up for a good marriage, and her aristocratic connections, her 'friends', would undoubtedly have been an added inducement to any would-be suitor. She would as a result have been groomed and clothed to attract a suitable match, and an attractive, vivacious, and quick-minded girl would not have gone short of admirers. It is difficult at this remove to be sure whether the young Ann, as a result, was over-indulged and spoilt, and therefore perhaps used to getting whatever she wanted; but it was the wayward and amoral Ann who was to become fatally entangled with Robert Foulkes.

Opposite: The ancient parish church of St. Tydecho at Mallwyd, in Merioneth. It is claimed that this site has been a place of worship since the sixth century. Here, on the 19th of February 1634, the infant Robert Foulkes was baptized, possibly by the rector Dr. John Davies. Foulkes will have remembered the oak porch being built during his boyhood, for the lintel is carved with the date 1641.

CHAPTER 4

Enter: Robert Foulkes

'God provided plentifully for me; by the favour of a noble and an honourable Patron I was setled very comfortably as to all the concerns of humane life'

Foulkes' main if dubious claim to a place in history is his eventual execution at Tyburn in January 1679 for murder, and it was to earn him an entry in the Dictionary of National Biography.[19] What irrational impulse should have brought a man of the Church to such a squalid end is almost beyond comprehension. Nonetheless, enough historical documents have survived to enable us to piece together the story of a conscientious parish priest and talented preacher, whose ministry was imperiled by the slide into self-indulgence that eventually led him to his doom. We know little of his beginnings, and until now it has long been assumed that he was a native of Shropshire. In fact Robert, whose father was also named Robert Foulkes, was born by his own account in Mallwyd, or Malloyd as he called it, a remote rural parish which includes Dinas Mawddwy, and straddles the county boundary between Montgomeryshire and Merioneth.[20] He was baptized on the 19th March 1633/34 in the ancient parish church of St. Tydecho; and while the name of his mother is never mentioned, an elder brother John was also baptized there in August 1631. If there were subsequent siblings we may never know of them, as the pages of the register between 1634 and 1658 are now missing.[21]

Although his family may not have been wealthy, he appears to have received a good local education; and during the twelve months following the 17th November 1648, Foulkes, apparently accompanied by his elder brother John, was admitted as a scholar at the Royal Free Grammar School at Shrewsbury. An admission fee of two shillings was charged for each boy, the standard fee for pupils 'borne without the countie of Salope'.[22] Indeed they will not have felt out of place, as there were at this time many native Welsh-speakers at the school. This prepared him to go up to Oxford University where he matriculated in November 1652.[23] Anthony à Wood, the eccentric antiquary and curmudgeon of Merton College, tells us that Foulkes had become a servitor at Christ Church in the autumn of 1651, 'where he continued more than four years, under the tuition and government of presbyterians and independents', subsequently becoming a preacher.[24] Despite what Wood considered decidedly dubious influences, Foulkes was obviously comfortable within the fold of the Established Church, where he said he had his birth and education, later claiming that he, 'by the Imposition of Episcopal hands, was in Anti-Episcopal times, ordained a Minister of his Holy Gospel.' These were almost certainly the hands of Dr. Robert Skinner, then former Bishop of Oxford, who had been ejected during the Commonwealth but, despite considerable risk, had continued to hold ordinations in secret.[25]

By the latter 1650s the 23-year-old Foulkes had returned to the borders of his native Wales, preaching in surrounding churches of which one may well have been Stanton Lacy, for living in the Atkinson household was a young woman of exactly his age who was to become his future wife. On the 7th September 1657, in Ludlow parish church, he married Isabella, daughter of Thomas Colbatch, a former Ludlow rector, who had died twenty years before when Isabella was a child aged three. Almost exactly three years later, following the Restoration and Lord Craven's return in triumph with the King, Foulkes was inducted as vicar at Stanton Lacy on

Shrewsbury School and the Castle gates, drawn in 1658, and only seven years after Foulkes had left for Oxford. During Foulkes' time, in August 1650, the school had been closed down for several months due to an outbreak of plague.

the 12th September 1660.[26] After a period of 'indispensible Absence' up until the end of 1661, he appears by the following year to have become comfortably settled in because one of his first recorded acts, in March 1662, was to contribute a 'free and voluntary present to his Majestie' King Charles the Second, who following his coronation was now seriously short of funds. Foulkes subscribed the sum of forty shillings, one of the largest contributions from the clergy in the diocese.[27]

Most of what follows in Foulkes' story is pieced together from the witness statements and depositions laid before the Bishop of Hereford's consistory court, held in Ludlow parish church, during the later 1670s.[28] The reader must remember that these statements, although taken under oath, cannot always be accepted at their face value. There is much contradiction, and we find that the oath of at least one of the parties just cannot be trusted. Each deposition has been made by a person with his or her own agenda, possibly under influence or pressure, and may have been 'spun' accordingly. Particularly when under oath, what the witnesses avoided saying is often as significant. Despite this fog of bias and evasion, a nonetheless fascinating story emerges.

Some of these papers briefly but intriguingly refer back to the early years of Foulkes' incumbency, and it seems that he and his young wife were lodged together for a time in Elizabeth Atkinson's house. Mrs. Atkinson, upon the death of her husband, succeeded to the lease and continued to occupy the farmhouse of what was then known as 'Hammonds' farm.[29]

We also learn, from evidence given later by Elizabeth, that the young Isabella Colbatch had been 'educated' by her, and lived with her 'for the greater part of her time from her infancy untill the time of her marriage, and for some time after'.[30] This statement at first sight does not seem to make

Ludstone Hall, at Claverley, is one of the finest Jacobean houses in Shropshire. It was built, supposedly in about 1607, by John Whitmore, Ann Atkinson's grandfather, on the site of the previous family home. Ann was reported to have stayed here with her uncle Thomas during the summer of 1674, while recuperating from childbirth.

sense because Elizabeth, according to her own testimony, did not arrive in Stanton Lacy until about 1654, when Isabella was already about 20 years of age. However, in law the term 'infancy' also means minority. It could also be that Isabella had already been part of the Atkinson household well before this time, perhaps from the age of fourteen, and continued living in their home to help care for the vicar's now motherless children.

Whatever the case may be, it seems that she was regarded virtually as part of the Atkinson household, certainly helping Elizabeth to care for the three young children after her husband's death. The reason for the newly married couple remaining there after their marriage was not made clear, although the most likely explanation is that, after Foulkes' induction, the original vicarage was then either still occupied by tenants, or was perhaps in the process of repair or rebuilding.[31] Foulkes subsequently moved back there, but he and Isabella appear to have remained childless for some eight years until their own daughter, Elizabeth, arrived in 1665.

It would have been at the time of his marriage that Robert Foulkes first encountered the late vicar's daughter Ann, she then being a child of about seven. The families may still have been living together as late as around 1662 when an incident occurred that was recalled by Ann's eldest brother, John Atkinson, during the court proceedings. Ann lost a diamond ring and suspected that Isabella had it, 'thereupon there happened some difference between them, and then Mistress Foulks complained that Ann was too fond of her husband'. Elizabeth Atkinson told John of Isabella's complaint, 'and they joyntly did chide Ann who denied what she was accused of'.[32] At this time, Ann would only have been about twelve years of age. Another statement asserted that by the time Ann was fifteen she was already 'very much conversant' with Foulkes, and often in his company.

Regarding further details of all this the documents remain frustratingly silent, and give us only glimpses of the relationships of the principal characters, leaving a multitude of questions unanswered. Was Foulkes, perhaps, a good-looking, charismatic young preacher, who naturally attracted attention and women? No portrait as far as we know has survived, but he does appear to have had a particular talent and following as a preacher. Was Ann indeed the spoilt youngest child, a pampered temperamental little girl used to having whatever she wanted? Perhaps bearing out this idea, another court statement mentioned Ann's obvious pleasure, in later years, in making Isabella jealous. She was said to have thrown her arms around Foulkes' neck and repeatedly kissed him in front of his wife, 'and then in a scornful manner askeinge [Foulkes] if [Isabella] were jealous, and tellinge her further that shee would give her greater cause for jealousy than kissing would doe, or used words to the same effect'.[33] Trying to put forward reasons for all this, on such fragmentary evidence, would be mere speculation, but it is likely that Isabella had played a significant part in raising Ann from her babyhood, and become closer to her than Elizabeth ever was. Isabella, by marrying Foulkes just five months after the death of Ann's father, had allowed him to come between them. To a bereaved seven-year-old girl, this may well have seemed like an act of betrayal. Had the Foulkes family not been so closely entangled with the Atkinson household, then things might have been very different, but this was not to be.

On the surface the first few years otherwise appear uneventful enough, although a difference between Foulkes and Elizabeth Atkinson over tithes and glebe, in 1667, was noted in the parish register.[34] Under the terms of her husband's will she had succeeded to the impropriation by lease of the township of Stanton Lacy – that is, she now took the great or rectoral tithe of corn and grain.[35] This difference with Foulkes, however, does not appear to have caused a significant rift between the parties, and all was evidently resolved amicably enough in his favour through mediators, by reference to her late husband's own records. In the meantime, Foulkes seems to have fulfilled his parochial duties and functions with little adverse comment on the part of his flock or associates. To sum up his position, in his own words:[36]

God provided plentifully for me; by the favour of a noble and an honourable Patron I was setled very comfortably as to all the concerns of humane life ... my portion was so far from being scanty, that I had enough and to spare, and (till late) I was beloved of my Parishioners, and respected in my Neighbourhood.'

At the end of August 1670 we know that he acted for Lady Martha Eure, the widow of lawyer Sir Sampson Eure. He had been a former Attorney General for Wales, a Member of Parliament for Leominster in 1640, and Speaker of the Oxford Parliament of 1644; but being a devoted royalist he suffered greatly under the Commonwealth, and died in about 1659. The Eures also had Stanton Lacy connections, in that they had been married in the parish church by John Whateley in June 1633.

Foulkes visited Lady Eure's home at Gatley Park, in the parish of Aymestrey, to 'discourse with her about severall businesses of her concernes, part whereof related unto the setling of her Estates & to the makeing of her last Will & Testament'. She had spoken several times to Foulkes about this, having cause to 'complaine of the unkindness of her owne relacions, especially of her brother', and now repeated 'some Instruccions which she had formerly given [Foulkes], & did desire [him] at the same time to draw her will, & gave speciall direccions & Instruccions for the doeing thereof'. Foulkes accordingly drew up the will in her presence, and it was this document, which is in his handwriting and still survives, that was later produced as evidence in a court case against her brother, Daniel Cage, in which the will was contested and Cage was sued for debt.[37] After it had been signed and witnessed, Lady Eure then gave the document into Foulkes' safekeeping, asking him 'to preserve the same, & after her decease to deliver it unto her Executor', George Lord Eure.

Not long after this, she and Lord Eure together called at Stanton Lacy vicarage so that he could read the will through, and then it was returned once more into Foulkes' care. Two years later, to Martha Eure's great distress, George Eure, 'the best friend she had in the world', died in London in October 1672, and Foulkes was again summoned to Gatley for consultations. Despite his attendance, the name of the executor was never actually altered in the will, although witnesses were to testify that Lady Eure did verbally name Lord Eure's brother, Ralph, as his successor. This was upheld when the will was proved, but conflicting witness statements as to other things she was alleged to have said gave the new Lord Eure grounds to contest two legacies of ten pounds each, one to Lady Eure's brother, and the other to her niece. Prolonged litigation ensued, in which Foulkes apparently played an active part on Lord Eure's behalf, and this was to make him enemies for the future.[38]

In the final clause of her will, however, Lady Eure had desired 'that Mr Robert Foulkes Vicar of Stanton Lacy, in the County of Salop, may preach my funerall Sermon & have mourneing & payment according to my Executors discretion'. This would support the impression that Foulkes was at this time held in a position of trust and respect among people of some position and influence. Indeed an 18th-century source, published over 50 years later, commented that Foulkes had been 'very much esteemed for his learning and abilities. Few men were more capable of shining in a church, or had a greater share of that sacred eloquence so requisite in a preacher. He was minister of Stanton Lacy... where he was exceedingly followed and admired till his crimes came to be known, and where he might have been beloved till death in a natural way had taken him hence, and then universally lamented, if his heart had been as well furnished with grace as his head was with knowledge and his tongue with expressions'.[39]

It must by now be evident that not all was well beneath the surface. One source may imply that all this had started before the birth of Foulkes' third child, between 1668 and

1670.[40] Certainly by 1673 the 40-year-old Foulkes was living a double life, and rumours were evidently circulating as early as 1674.[41] Shortly before Christmas 1675 Ann Atkinson, still a spinster at 25, returned after a prolonged period away from Stanton Lacy, apparently having stayed with relatives in London and elsewhere.[42]

The first public sign that something was wrong only seems to have become obvious to one of Foulkes' parishioners during the following summer, in 1676. George Coston, a local farmer, was coming out of church one Sunday after hearing Foulkes deliver a sermon upon a text from James' Epistle iv. 7: 'Resist the Devil, and he will fly from thee.' A certain William Hopton, recently become landlord of the local tavern, was heard to say very publicly: 'What discourse have we had about the devil'; and pointing to Ann, added: 'There the she-devil goes, let *him* resist *her!*'[43]

THE HOPTONS

Publican William Hopton emerges as the key figure and prime mover in the parish's harassment of Robert Foulkes, but he was clearly an unprincipled rogue, a vindictive troublemaker, and the worst sort of man to cross. He was born in Stanton Lacy of minor gentry or yeoman stock in about 1651, son of Richard Hopton senior (1621–1690), and younger brother of Richard Hopton junior (1642–1715). Robert Foulkes not only fell out with William, but with his father and brother as well.

It also seems that William might have been a chip off the old block, for the seeds of the Hoptons' warfare with Foulkes were apparently sown at a time when Richard Hopton senior was a churchwarden, an office he had served on at least seven occasions between 1651 and 1673. Richard held £10 in trust, part of a 'stock of money which belonged to the poore of the parish', which when enquired after, he maintained had been put in the hands of a John Knight, who previously had served as a churchwarden before the Civil War. Knight was however now dead, and Hopton had made pretence of suing his widow for the money, at the cost of the parish. When the parishioners enquired of the widow, she maintained that she was not being sued by Hopton at all, and that anyway the money had long since been repaid to Hopton by her late husband.

Hopton was very publicly rebuked by Foulkes from the pulpit and, apparently with the vicar's encouragement, the parishioners presented him before the consistory court, which in turn referred the matter to the Justices of the Peace. They, according to Foulkes, established that the money was all the time in Hopton's hands, although up until then he had stubbornly refused to repay it. In later testimony his sons were still in denial about the matter, even though its eventual repayment by Hopton, in June 1676, had been carefully noted in the parish register.[44]

Foulkes' obligations as trustee and adviser to his parishioners were now to bring him into yet further conflict with the Hoptons, who later accused him of being 'a turbulent and contentious man, and one that occasioned severall vexatious suites of law amongst his neighbours and parishoners', and more particularly that he had created a 'difference' between Richard Hopton the younger and his father-in-law. This last, according to Foulkes, came about because William Hopton was being employed as a bailiff or steward to the now Earl of Craven, collecting certain rents from the tenants on his estate. Richard Hopton senior, and William's elder brother Richard junior, had been obliged to enter into a bond as guarantors for William's 'faythfull service' and honest conduct in his duties. It seems however that William's more questionable tendencies were already a matter of some concern among his wider family. His elder brother's father-in-law, Nicholas Tippen, perhaps on behalf of his daughter Hannah, entreated Foulkes to speak with Richard Hopton junior to get himself released from the bond, 'tellinge him the danger he stoode in in case there was any miscariage committed by his sayd brother William. And the sayd Richard Hopton acquaintinge his father of what councell and advice' he had received from Foulkes, later cited this incident as evidence of Foulkes' attempt to create discord between the family members.

From this it is abundantly clear that Richard the younger resented Foulkes' interference just as much as his brother and father. However, in the light of subsequent events, he almost certainly came to regret bitterly not having taken the vicar's advice, for by the end of 1677 William appears to have absconded with a large sum of Lord Craven's money, and Richard found himself bound by the bond, and 'forced to confess judgment' for the debt.[45]

William Hopton's capacity for intrigue and skulduggery first showed itself in a way that directly involved several members of the Atkinson family. Elizabeth, as previously mentioned, was the impropriator by lease of Stanton Lacy township, held of Lord Craven, also enjoying the lease of Hammonds farm. Both of these leases she had succeeded to on her husband's death, to enjoy during the period of her lifetime.

On her death, the farm lease would have reverted to her stepson Francis Atkinson, the parson, while the lease of the impropriation was to pass to her stepdaughter Ann. According to Foulkes' account, William Hopton as bailiff to Lord Craven now took it upon himself to 'earnestly solliscit the sayd Earl and his commissioners for new leases, and that the life of one Mary Wythers, the neece, and daughter to the brother of the sayd Elizabeth, should be put into the sayd leases' in their place, Hopton pretending to his lordship's commissioners that Francis Atkinson was going to marry Mary.[46] For the 'better confirmation' of this concocted story, Hopton had somehow persuaded Isabella Foulkes to 'forge' certain letters to Lord Craven and his commissioners in Elizabeth's name, as a result of which, although in defiance of the explicit provisions of Thomas Atkinson's will, new leases were duly granted for the life of Mary Withers. No sooner were these leases obtained than the 20-year-old Mary absconded from Elizabeth's house, and Hopton now married her himself!

Our knowledge of this blatant fraud comes to us in Robert Foulkes' own words, and it is also mentioned by Elizabeth Atkinson, although whether Isabella was motivated to collude in Hopton's scheme by the thought of her depriving her husband's mistress, and did so with enthusiasm or only after persuasion, is never enlarged upon. When all this came to the ears of Ann at her return at Christmas 1675, after about two years of absence, she went to her cousin, Lord Craven, and complained to him that she had been utterly undone by Hopton's 'fraudulent and unjust dealings, and Lord Craven beinge made to understand the truth thereof forced Hopton to cancell the sayd new leases which he had procured in the name of Wythers, which disapoynment soe vexed Hopton and his wife that they vowed to be revenged against Mistress Anne Attkinson'.[47] Rather surprisingly, there is no mention of Hopton being disciplined at this time by his employer for his actions, but his propensity for scheming and corruption was eventually to lead to his downfall.

What is most likely a fair summary of Hopton's character is provided by Foulkes himself among his defence statements. While noting Foulkes' understandable prejudice in these opinions, and that it is at least in part a case of pot calling kettle black, his graphic character reference is probably not far from the truth:

> William Hopton ... is a person of a viciouse scandalouse and licentious life and conversation, and one who is publiquely reported and knowne for a common drunkard, lyer and swearer, and hath ... gloryed in his debauchery, and confessed that he had a bastard childe, and hath publiquely acknowledged it himself and proclaymed it two severall Sundayes in the church yard at Staunton Lacy ... and [he is] one that is a constant sabath breaker, sellinge his ale on the Lordes day and makinge people drunke, and then quarrellinge beatinge and abusing of them, and causinge them to reare the cry to the greate disturbance of the church, and hath often times swore God damne him, but he would out the vicar of Staunton Lacy or he would not stay in the parish or countrey himself, meaninge thereby that he would cause the said Mr Foulkes to be deprived of his vicaridge, actinge in this particular meerely out of hatred and mallice, saying revenge is sweet, and for a mallicious vexatious and turbulent person he is commonly accompted reputed and taken '

That the 24-year-old Hopton did undoubtedly have an illegitimate son is supported by other evidence laid before the court, and John Atkinson related how Hopton had had a fling with 'one Symonds, a coffy mans maid at Grais [Grays] Inn back Gate in London'. Samuel Brompton, the solicitor who acted for Hopton, reported that he had 'compounded' or negotiated a settlement of five pounds for the matter, which he said 'was the cheapest that ever any such thing was donn for in London'![48]

It was, however, one thing for a young single layman and mere sinner to sow his wild oats, but quite another matter for a married man of the Church; and it was at around the time of his courtship and marriage with Mary Withers that Hopton discovered a family secret, and confirmed the rumours he had been hearing for some little time. Being Elizabeth's niece, Mary had been living with her at Hammond's Farm, apparently since the age of about nine, and so was not only witness to the goings-on in the house but was certainly intimate with some of the family's more sensitive confidences. This gave Hopton inside information about a hushed-up affair between Foulkes and Ann.

What was more, it had not been a passing flirtation, for in 1673 there had been a pregnancy, and 23-year-old Ann had been sent away for about six months to the house of a neighbour near to her elder brother Francis, who was by then curate at West Felton near Oswestry in northern Shropshire. There a baby girl had been born, in about May of 1674, after which Ann briefly returned to Stanton Lacy, only to be shortly afterwards packed off to her uncle near Bridgnorth, and then to a relative in London, so that the whole thing could be given a chance to blow over. Furthermore, it had been Mary Withers who had been dispatched to West Felton by Elizabeth to fetch Ann home.[49] On her arrival there, Mary found Ann in a very weak condition, barely able to stand unaided; and she noticed Ann constantly applying a green ointment to her breast, probably some preparation to help suppress breast-milk.[50] Ann had also been visited by Foulkes, who had stayed for two days, bringing with him 'wyne and sweet meats, and two sheets of pinns'.

Mary also recalled that, before Ann had ever left for West Felton, she had seen her sewing several pieces of child linen, claiming that she was making them for a relative.

The Hoptons had other sources of information as well. As early as October 1674, Richard Hopton the younger had overheard a certain Elias Greaves haranguing Foulkes about the pregnancy; and about six months later Isabella told him that she had only become aware of the existence of the child when she discovered letters between Ann and her husband talking of financial provision for the baby's maintenance. Foulkes, it seems, had paid twenty pounds in three installments to Ann's brother

Francis, who evidently took in hand the arrangements at the West Felton end. Furthermore, Foulkes had also confessed to Isabella's brother, John Colbatch, about the pregnancy, although he later denied ever doing so.[51]

With Ann now out of the way in London, she had been unable to keep an eye on her affairs and interests at home, and Hopton and Mary had made their plans. They had almost certainly talked at length with Isabella Foulkes about her husband's affair, and the forging of the letters in Elizabeth's name was evidently a chance for Isabella to be revenged on Ann and her brother, Francis. Whatever the facts, with Ann's final return at Christmas in 1675, and the overturning of William Hopton's carefully laid scheme, the frustrated and now embittered publican decided to set about gathering hard evidence to expose publicly the lovers' affair, now openly declaring that he would have Foulkes turned out of his vicarage for his indiscretion.

Opposite: The large Bronze Age round-barrow, known as Robin Hood's Butt, or Butt Tump, that stands on the edge of Old Field, at the southwest corner of Stanton Lacy parish. Now covered with trees, it is a prominent feature in the local landscape and, despite a fairly primitive excavation in 1884, still stands to a height of over four metres. It also marks the parish's boundary with Bromfield and, together with an ancient sycamore tree that once crowned it, was mentioned in an agreement set down in the parish register in 1695 by Foulkes' successor, Samuel Newborough. Widow Partridge's bowling green lay 200 yards to the south, where the golf club is today.

Robin Hood, according to legend, once stood upon this mound, and let fly an arrow which hit the tower of Ludlow parish church, a mere two and a half miles away. An iron arrow, said to commemorate the shot, is still set in the roof of the north transept, although in fact it formerly marked the Fletchers' or arrowmakers' chancel.

CHAPTER 5

Vox Populi

'It burst out with that violence, like water long damned up, that all took notice of it... and what I thought to be an Arcanum between my partner and my self, is now become Vox populi; the Neighbourhood rings and ecchoes again with it.'

SOME SLEUTHING

And so it was in June 1676 that William Hopton, and a Charles Pearce of Eastfields in the parish, whom he had persuaded to accompany him, set off together for northern Shropshire to try to uncover the full facts about Ann's delivery three years previously, and discover the present whereabouts of the child.

They first called on a John Garbett, who, while originally a native of Stanton Lacy, was a merchant who had lived at Shrewsbury for some twenty years before moving on to Whittington, near Oswestry. Here Hopton and Pearce grilled the unfortunate Garbett and his wife for two or three hours to find out whether they knew anything of an illegitimate child, which they emphatically denied ever having heard of, whereupon Hopton promised them five pounds if they could unearth any information about where the child might now be found. Garbett in exasperation retorted that for five pounds he would willingly bring him any child. Hopton answered that 'if he would bring him to Foulks his child, begotten on Mistress Atkinson, he should have it, to which [Garbett] replyed that he knew of none she had'. While in the neighbourhood, Hopton and Pearce also appear to have called on the London merchant Thomas Lloyd of Whittington Castle, at one time a suitor for Ann's hand, who was informed by Hopton that Foulkes had deflowered her when she was but twelve years old![52]

Hopton then rode on to West Felton where he confronted the rector, the august Dr. William Bradley, and 'did much inveigh against Mr Francis Atkinson as being unjust upon some accompts between them concerning the Lord Craven's business, and alsoe did raile against his sister Mistress Ann Atkinson, and talked very scandalously of Mr Robert Foulks... saying that Mistress Ann Atkinson had a bastard, and the said Mr Foulks was the father of it, and that she was delivered thereof in West Felton house'.[53]

Bradley simply told him that if this was indeed the truth then he should be very glad to see it out in the open, but 'bid him take care of what he said for that these words were very scandalous and of dangerous consequence if he should fail in proveing them.' Hopton retorted that he was now resolved to make the matter public, and would do as much as he could to have Foulkes either silenced or deprived of his living. On being asked what good he would gain from this, Hopton had merely replied 'Revenge is sweet', a phrase he was to repeat on several occasions.

If the results of Hopton's and Pearce's findings were formally written down at the time they have not survived, but two years later a hearing was conducted at West Felton before a local Justice of the Peace, Robert Owen, at his home called Woodhouse, at which Pearce and Richard Hopton senior were both present. This had been at the instigation of Hopton senior, and a warrant had been granted to make further enquiries.

These took place at the end of June 1678, not only to establish whether a child had been born to Ann Atkinson, but on the pretext of finding out whether or not it might have been murdered. It seems that suspicion had arisen, perhaps because the child's whereabouts were being so resolutely concealed.

There are variations in the resulting story among the several sources, but it appears that in late 1673 Ann had been 'carried' to West Felton and was received at the house of an Edward Walker, yet another native of Stanton Lacy, where lodging had been arranged for her, and she had stayed for about six months. The investigation then established by verbal testimony that Mary Owen, a local midwife, assisted by two other women, delivered a baby girl either there or at the parsonage house. She was then baptized by Francis Atkinson and given the name of Ann, and two days later sent away to nurse over the Welsh border.

On enquiry, the child was found to be alive and well 'at the house of one Brey' at Llansantffraid in Montgomeryshire, a mere nine miles away, and living under the name of Mary Morris, supported by an allowance of five pounds a year towards which Ann contributed at least part.[54]

Hopton and Pearce must have confirmed most of this story in June 1676 at the time of their journey; and Pearce later said he had on that occasion seen the child, even claiming to have taken a lock of her hair.[55] Nonetheless, before returning to Stanton Lacy, both called in again on John Garbett at Whittington to inform him that they had now found out where the child was and so were no longer 'beholden' to him, although they still pressed him again for over an hour for yet more information, despite his repeated protestations that he still knew nothing.

Following the investigators' return, the Hoptons now grasped their 'longe waited for' opportunity to get at Foulkes, and were assisted by another ally, Richard Chearme, a yeoman, whom they may have been instrumental in helping to elect at the previous Easter as one of the churchwardens. Chearme also happened to be Elizabeth Atkinson's tenant at Hammonds farm at a rent of £58 10s. a year, occupying with his wife Margaret part of Elizabeth's house. He had been born at High Ercall in about 1629 and was a relative newcomer, living latterly at Whitton in the parish of Burford for some six years, before arriving in Stanton Lacy in May 1674.[56] Despite his dependence upon the Atkinsons, as churchwarden Chearme seems to have had no reservations in presenting his vicar before the Bishop of Hereford.

BEFORE THE BISHOP

'... at Croft Castle in the County of Hereford before the Right Reverend in God Herbert, Lord Bishopp of Hereford, there was a Complaint made to the said Lord Bishopp against Robert Foulks, touching and concerning his associating himselfe with and keeping company with Ann Atkinson at unseasonable times and in private places ...'

The scene now briefly shifts to Croft Castle in Herefordshire, which, after demolition during the Civil War, had been completely rebuilt during the early 1660s as a rural retreat and episcopal palace by the new bishop, Dr. Herbert Croft, who was also heir to the estate. At one of his audience court sessions at the castle, the bishop was informed of the situation during the following month, July 1676, when 'severall of the Inhabitants of Stanton Lacy' complained of the 'divers crimes and misdemeanours' committed by Foulkes. Those attending

Above: Croft Castle and its parish church, from the south-west. Bishop Herbert Croft, as eldest surviving son and heir to the Croft estate, rebuilt the castle just after the Restoration as his own episcopal palace, its predecessor having been totally dismantled by the Royalists in 1645. Here Robert Foulkes was summoned by his bishop in July 1676 to receive his admonition. The castle was later substantially remodelled during the 18th-century.
The parish church of St. Michael, seen on the right, is the last remnant of the medieval buildings.

this meeting certainly included Chearme, as churchwarden, and also Elizabeth Atkinson, who with others was in dispute with the bishop over tithes; and on that occasion, Dr. Croft questioned the witnesses present before adjourning his enquiry until the following week. That the vicar was there at this first session is unlikely, for the bishop now sent a written order via Chearme to Foulkes to appear before him at the next meeting to answer the charges, and this the churchwarden duly delivered to the vicarage on the following Sunday morning. It was at this second session at Croft that Foulkes was personally admonished by his bishop to avoid any further contact with Ann, unless at least three or four other people of repute were present. Chearme, however, had been unable to attend again at the Castle, he said, 'by reason of a blow' which his vicar had given him a few days before.

By the midsummer of 1676 Foulkes' behaviour had become curiously uninhibited to the point of being outrageous. Seemingly infuriated that anyone should presume to disapprove of an already-married 42-year-old parson becoming infatuated with a 26-year-old parishioner, and apparently careless of the effect upon his unfortunate wife, he was on occasion even openly demonstrative with Ann, particularly when in Elizabeth's house.

Looking out one day from Elizabeth's parlour window to see Isabella passing by, he said to Ann: 'See how my wife looketh malice and envy'; and chucking Ann under her chin remarked: 'Jealousie will eat her up, and I will keep her short enough, and keep it all for thee'.

This was said quite openly in the presence of a parishioner, Martha Dovey. Martha also related how, some months before, Foulkes had told Ann to tell her 'what she had donn with the little thing she had at West Felton', to which Ann had pertly told him 'to tell it himselfe, for it as much concern'd him as her'![57]

This forceful oil portrait of Bishop Herbert Croft (1603–1691) hangs at Croft Castle, in Herefordshire, and was probably painted at about the time of Foulkes' encounter with him. It portrays well the face by which Foulkes was confronted, when he was summoned in July 1676 to be admonished for his conduct. He holds in one hand the Book of Common Prayer, and despite his rather severe countenance Croft was said to have been a warm, devout man, who spent much of his time at the castle in preference to the bishop's palace in Hereford. (*Reproduced by courtesy of the National Trust*).

It was at around the time of the delivery of the bishop's summons, at the end of July, that Foulkes totally lost his self-control, not only attacking Isabella but also assaulting Chearme with a pair of fire tongs. This was no doubt as a result of the mounting pressure upon Foulkes, who was now only too well aware of what was being stirred up against him. Thus it first appears that, when provoked, the vicar did indeed have an explosively violent side to his character, although the Chearmes later convinced themselves that he had deliberately set it up.

AN EVENING AT THE VICARAGE

There had been rather more obvious changes in Foulkes' general behaviour that cannot have escaped notice and comment among his parishioners, particularly his increasing patronage of at least one local hostelry, and he was later to write:

> I remember the time, and I believe 'tis not forgot in my late Neighbourhood, when I had a very competent share of temperance and sobriety; I can truly attest, that an Alehouse or a Tavern had none, or but very little of my custome...

By the summer of 1676 all that had changed, for a day or two before receiving the bishop's admonition, Foulkes had gone to drink and play bowls at the alehouse and bowling green of widow Anne Partridge on the Old Field, just over the Bromfield parish boundary. Here he was approached by the vicar of Bromfield, John Slade, who privately told him of his concern about the rumours circulating locally, and gently asked him to avoid Ann's company. This well-meaning advice, at least in Slade's presence, Foulkes apparently received 'very kindly and quietly', although once the vicar was out of earshot

Foulkes appears to have become 'angry and much offended' at his interference, and towards evening he returned home 'distempered with drinking', evidently suspecting that it was Isabella who had complained to John Slade.[58] On reaching the vicarage, Foulkes sent for a neighbour, Francis Underwood, and then for Richard Chearme, who could not at first be found because he was out late haymaking with his labourers in the fields. As soon as both men were there, Foulkes called for more liquor, and then drank to Chearme's health 'with much seeming kindness'; and then sent for the men's wives to join them all for supper, and 'for some time was very pleasant with them'.

This was the agreeable prelude to what was to become an evening of mayhem centred around one man, and it was after about an hour that Foulkes, now clearly much the worse for wear, started behaving badly. First he grabbed hold of Margaret Chearme, 'and laying his hand upon her belly said that she was a lean scragg, all bones, and said that he would not hurt his prick with such a person'! Then he laid hold of Judith Underwood, 'and putting his hand on her belly said that there was good flesh and, takeing her upon his lapp, thrust his hand under her coats and lifted them up unto her knees, at which she was offended and gott from him', and at this point both she and her husband prudently decided to leave. Margaret Chearme, perceiving that Foulkes was in an 'untoward humour', now asked her husband whether they too might go home, upon which Foulkes promptly lost his temper. He rounded on Margaret, accusing her of spreading a story that he and Ann had been seen together in a 'bower', which she denied, at which he told her to 'goe play the whore with William Hopton and his wife'. He then informed Margaret and Isabella that both of them were Hopton's whores, suggesting that 'comeing from Ludlow upon Old Field they were both his whores there, and that one held the horses whilst the other was served or occupied'! Foulkes was markedly free with his use of the word 'whore', and yet he seems to have used it more to shock and scandalize than to be taken seriously – indeed it seems most likely that he had simply made up the story on the spur of the moment. Despite this, Margaret Chearme later said that resulting from Foulkes' accusation, she and her husband fell out for a time. For his next insult, Foulkes now told Chearme he was a 'Rogue and Cuckold', at which Isabella decided to withdraw up to her room, while the churchwarden and his wife beat a hasty retreat.[59]

On leaving the vicarage, the Chearmes now found a small group gathering outside, attracted by the shouting within, but they were not there long before Isabella was heard to shriek and cry out several times. A graphic account of what happened next was the core of a direct accusation among the court presentments:[60]

> ...you fell out and quarrelled with your wife and without any cause or provocacion called her whore, base whore, bitch, and other diffamatory names, and then beate, struck, and wounded her about the face, eyes, and head with your fiste and with a paire of iron tonges, and haveinge a penknife in your hand threattened to kill her or to be the death of her, and ... soe vyolent was your rage behaviour and actions against your wife, that a constable was called for to preserve her from your fury, and when the constable came soe fearefull was your wife and in such a trembleinge condicion, by reason of your threatts and terrible acts and execracions against her, that shee desired and begged the constable, for Gods sake, to stay with her or to sett a watch upon the house and to assist her that night untill the day came that shee might provide for herselfe and safety, and the constable att the request of your wife did sett a watch att your house which continewed there untill about six of the clock next morninge...

So violent was Foulkes' assault on his wife that Joan Wood, their maidservant, came running out of the house to beg the by-standers to come in and prevent Foulkes from killing Isabella, as she dared not come between them herself. The Constable being away, his deputy was duly summoned; and after charging Chearme and William Hopton to assist him, he knocked at the vicarage door only to be received by Foulkes who asked them what business they had there. They answered that they had heard an outcry from the house, and 'supposed it to be his wife', at which Foulkes coolly invited them in.

The Constable and Chearme entered the house to find Isabella in an upstairs room bruised and bleeding, and sitting weeping on a chair. Meanwhile Foulkes, with a pair of iron tongs in his hand, stood at the front door and menacingly invited Hopton to come in as well, at which Hopton warily declined, only to receive a torrent of abuse. For Foulkes, in his highly volatile state, and seeing the Constable accompanied by his arch-tormenters and accusers, it was clearly more than he could endure. The narrative continues:

> ...att the same tyme, when the constable came to the releife of your said wife, hee brought with him one Richard Cherme churchwarden of Staunton Lacy and one William Hopton gent. of the same parish, whom hee charged to assist and ayde him in the execucion of his office, with whome, upon enteringe your house by the said constables order, you in a most violent and passionate way fell out, curseinge and sweareinge att them, and after you had uttered severall horrible and abhominable oathes and execracions against them ... as By God, Gods Blood, God Dammee, and the like, att length you called them or one of them Rogues, Damned Doggs, sonnes of whores, Cuckolde, and the like names, and told them they were damned, and haveinge a paire of iron tonges in your hande struck the said Richard Cherme on the back or shoulder with them, insoemuch

that it made a wounde or scarr to arise thereon to the great offence of Almighty God, [and] the hurte and prejudice of the said Richard Cherme...

Foulkes had tried to push the churchwarden down some stairs, and struck him with the tongs on his elbow, but Chearme had managed to save himself by holding on to a beam, only to bump his head. Undaunted, as Chearme departed from the house, Foulkes then aimed another blow at the churchwarden's skull which missed, striking his shoulder. This broke the skin and caused severe bruising, the victim complaining that he was unable to use his arm for several days. Having driven Chearme from the house, Foulkes then went in search of his penknife, causing the maid to come running out a second time to sound the alarm, and thereafter the watch had been set and peace restored.

Later, Foulkes was to claim that Chearme's wound cannot have been all that severe because he was observed on the following day winnowing grain for a couple of hours in his barn. Nevertheless, in losing his self-control so disgracefully, Foulkes had merely played into the hands of his accusers; and this episode with the fire-tongs may help to explain Chearme's subsequent intense hostility towards him, revealed in later testimony. The situation also brings to mind the attack by Ralph Clayton, Foulkes' predecessor, upon his unfortunate sexton in the church some forty years before. For the few with memories long enough, it may well have seemed that history might now be repeating itself.

Opposite: The interior of Ludlow Castle as it looked in Foulkes' day, drawn in 1684 by Thomas Dineley. The drawbridge and the wall around the inner ditch have long since gone, and the fine buildings now stand roofless and abandoned to the sky. After the abolition of the Court in the Marches in 1689, the castle suffered over a century of depredation and neglect to become the ivy-covered romantic ruin beloved of Victorian photographers.

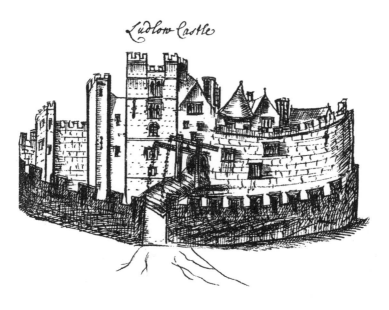

Ludlow Castle

CHAPTER 6

The Case Against Foulkes

'To this I opposed my confident denials, and those confirmed with Oaths and Execrations, which I too frequently used for my own purgation. I stood upon points and forms of Law, which I thought would have born me out.'

BEFORE THE COURT

This was to mark the beginning of a protracted and expensive ordeal for Foulkes. Proceedings against him did not stop with the bishop's admonition; and on the 1st August 1676 he was presented before the consistory court to 'answear to such articles as shall bee objected against him concerning his soules health, and the reformacion of his manners'.[61] In order

51

to do this, although being brought in the name of the church authorities, those pursuing this action first needed to find a sponsor or 'promoter' who would act as a guarantor of any costs, and yet was not directly involved in the proceedings. The unfortunate man chosen by the Hoptons was a cousin, one Francis Hutchinson, who had moved to Stanton Lacy as tenant at the Pools Farm only six weeks before he was approached on the matter. He later ruefully accounted for his involvement:

> ... at the first promocion of those articles against Robert Foulkes I was a strainger both to the person and the accions of the sayd Mr Foulkes, and ... I did not know then nor doe I know now any harme or evill of him, but I was instigated and inveigled thereinto by the importunate sollicitations of other persons who were then, and (as I believe) are yet, malliciously bent against the sayd Mr Foulkes, in particular by William Hopton of Staunton Lacy, ale seller, and Richard Hopton junior, his brother, both my relacions. These Hoptons, to perswade mee against the sayd Mr Foulks, told mee they had five or six goode stakes in the hedge, meaninge thereby five or six able and substantiall persons who would stick to mee in the managinge of that suite against Mr Foulkes, beare all the charges of it, [and] defende and indemnify mee from all advantages that Mr Foulkes might have against mee for and by reason of the said prosecution.

The 'substantiall persons' involved were the brothers William and Richard Hopton, Richard Chearme the churchwarden, a Joseph Dovey the elder and Martha his 'supposed' wife (also known as Martha Hawkes, from her first marriage), and Richard Wredenhall of Downton.

Joseph Dovey was a yeoman, born in the parish of Quatt in about 1622, who had moved to Stanton Lacy in around 1668. His inclusion among Foulkes' persecutors appears to have come about because Dovey bore a grudge against

Foulkes, who had become involved in a legal action against Dovey's wife Martha, to recover some money she had been bequeathed out of the estate of her late aunt, Lady Martha Eure of Gatley Park.[62] Dovey maintained that Foulkes had actually 'promoted and encouraged' this suit 'in the name of Lord Eure', and it had become a protracted legal process lasting some two to three years, only finally concluding in late 1676. There were also doubts among many about the validity of Dovey's declared marriage to Martha, formerly a widow, and Foulkes later referred to this and the legal action in his evidence:

> Joseph Dovey and Martha his pretended wife ... are persons of a very Ill fame and Reputacion, and reported formerly to have Lived for many years together in fornication and to have begotten one or more bastard Children, and ... Dovey and his sayd pretended wife still continue as is supposed soe to doe, theyre marriage beinge not as yet fully proved by any witnesses but the oath of the sayd Doveys pretended wife, wherein she hath sworne fraudulently and deceitfully, and whereas theyre sayd pretended testimony or certificate beares date at least six or seaven yeares last past, Dovey the sayd pretended husband was within two yeares last past with a person in Bridgenorth to Desire him to goe alonge with him to the Official of that peculiar Jurisdiccion to procure a Lycence for him to be marryed to Martha, his now pretended wife, soe that in all probability they are yet unmarryed but still Continue theyre filthy and uncleane Copulacions. Martha since the time of her pretended marriage, being sued at law as a feme sole, pleaded thereunto without any mention of her Coverture...[63]

This last comment refers to the apparently successful action to recover money in the name of Ralph, Lord Eure, in that it had named Martha Hawkes, widow, as a 'feme sole', that is a woman without husband, and independent as regards her property.[64]

Martha, although now supposedly married, did not deny such status, nor mentioned being under the protection of her new husband, leaving the question of their 'declared' relationship very much open to speculation.[65] Moreover, and much more damningly, Joseph Dovey had 'upon a Faire day' in Bridgnorth in 1674 gone to the shop of Luke Milner, a prominent local butcher, to persuade him to accompany and vouch for him in applying for a marriage licence from the Judge or Official of the Royal Peculiar Jurisdiction of Bridgnorth.[66] All this had taken place some three years after Martha had sworn an affidavit to say she was already married to him. Had Dovey now opted to marry in Stanton Lacy, this would have been as good as a public declaration that he was indeed cohabiting with Martha illegally and so, to save face and confound the doubters once and for all, Dovey had resolved to marry her in secret by licence in a jurisdiction and parish outside the diocese of Hereford. Dovey however, perhaps to preserve his anonymity, would not reveal to Milner who his intended wife was; and so the cautious Milner, knowing that he would be drawn into signing a bond or monetary guarantee as to Dovey's good faith, refused to support him, to the would-be groom's evident frustration.

The other named supporter of, and contributor to, the action against Foulkes was Richard Wredenhall, a gentleman, who had served as a churchwarden in 1675, the year before Chearme. No statements were ever taken from him, and he is a rather shadowy figure, remaining relatively on the fringe of these proceedings; but he gave Hopton encouragement by dipping into his pocket on one occasion to present him with twenty shillings towards the court costs. Hutchinson said that Wredenhall had 'private whisperinge and conference' with the Hoptons, acting in part as a legal adviser, informing them that had they acted as promoters themselves, then they would not have been able to give evidence as witnesses. It was because of this advice that they had approached Hutchinson.

Wredenhall was nonetheless cited at one point as a defence alibi, during the time he was a churchwarden. In 1675 Foulkes had celebrated Christmas with Andrew Walker at Whitbach, staying overnight with Wredenhall at Downton, although rumour had suggested he had been with Ann Atkinson at Elizabeth's house.[67] Isabella at this time was apparently away in Worcester, where her elder brother, the prosperous mercer William Colbatch, lived in the parish of St Swithun's.

This consortium of accusers now retained Richard Cornwall of Brimfield Cross, a notary public, as their 'proctor' or legal counsel, who also assured the newcomer Hutchinson that his only involvement would be in 'deliveringe in a paper which (he sayd) any body might doe without danger'. This first document, under fourteen 'articles' or headings, was placed before the court on the 1st August 1676, in the name of Hutchinson although not actually bearing his signature. Indeed he later maintained that these articles were 'never wholly reade to mee, nor did I know what was contained in some of them'. It was followed, however, not long afterwards by an additional list of seven articles, dated the 28th of November, which was signed by him.[68]

Chearme's formal presentation of Foulkes before the Court, marked simply with his initial R, was made on the 29th August 1676. It is but a brief document summarizing the charges, but adding for good measure a sting in its tail by alleging that Foulkes also 'doth suffer his house and barnes to goe out of repaire'![69]

OF ACCUSATIONS, AND SANCTIONS

The first 'article' merely set the scene by establishing that Foulkes was a priest in holy orders, and vicar of Stanton Lacy in the diocese of Hereford, and therefore was within the jurisdiction of the bishop's court. The second continued by asserting that as such, Foulkes should have behaved himself 'meekely, loveingly and friendly', and have been 'an example of love, humility, and charity to all men'.

Despite this, it declared, he had a 'turbulent, quarrelsome, and contentious spirit', and was constantly endeavouring to disturb the peace and quiet of his neighbours and parishioners by 'stirringe upp and promoteing vexacious suites of law and other troubles that might utterly destroy them and their families', and that for such a person he was commonly taken and reputed in the parish.

While it is already plain that Foulkes had succeeded, perhaps not always intentionally, in antagonizing some of his accusers, particularly the Hoptons and the Doveys, witnesses testifying in his defence do put a rather different gloss on his character.

Somerset Wall, a yeoman, said how Foulkes had 'composed severall differences' between him and his neighbours, the Underwoods, as also between a Richard Garbett and his son, 'always endeavouring ... to preserve peace and unity amongst his parishioners and disswadeing them from suits and contentions, and hath himselfe been an example of love and peace unto his neighbours, and for such a person... he hath been and is commonly reputed and taken to be by all persons that were or are acquainted with him, except by some who are concerneing in this suite'.

Richard Garbett senior confirmed that Foulkes had indeed resolved a quarrel between himself and his son; and the farmer George Coston related how he had quieted and composed 'a suite of law or controversie' between himself and a Thomas Garner.[70]

In this light it does appear that in the past Foulkes had in fact done much to defuse tensions and resolve disputes within his community, as indeed was his duty as a parish priest.

It therefore seems somewhat at odds with his own defence that Foulkes had, at the same time, embarked upon legal actions against four parishioners, three of whom just happened to be among his accusers – Hutchinson, Chearme, and Dovey. The lawsuits were about the payment of tithes in hay and wool, Foulkes complaining that he had only received customary payments in money that, due to inflation, were now a fraction of what the actual 'tenth' was worth in kind, and therefore 'much to his prejudice'. The defence simply argued that these payments had long been established by the vicar's predecessors and that, up until now, Foulkes had appeared happy enough to settle for the customary amounts.

Evidence from witnesses suggested, nonetheless, that Dovey had actually evaded paying tithes, in wool and hemp. Even though commuted to a fraction of their true value, tithes were ever unpopular with the farming community; and the more radical 17th-century sects, such as Quakers and Fifth-Monarchy Men, had vigorously opposed them, although no nonconformists are recorded in the parish in Foulkes' day.[71] Resentment against tithes, however, was less directed against the incumbent than against the institution that he represented; although if the parson was unpopular it would perhaps manifest itself rather more readily. At best, the yeoman's attitude was one of sullen acceptance, no doubt amply summed up in John Dryden's libretto to Henry Purcell's opera *King Arthur*, written just five years after Foulkes' death:

We've cheated the parson, we'll cheat him again
For why should a blockhead have one in ten?
One in ten, one in ten,
For why should a blockhead have one in ten?
For why should a blockhead have one in ten![72]

It continues:

> For prating so long like a book-learned sot,
> 'til pudding and dumpling are burned to the pot,
> burned to pot, burned to pot, etc.

Not all the court papers may have survived, nor do we know the outcome, but it is evident that Foulkes, who cannot have had much of a case, was using legal action chiefly as a weapon to intimidate his accusers by demanding his pound of flesh. Indeed, he himself later admitted that the 'securing or regaining of the Churches Rights, was the answer wherewith I stopped the mouths of all objections'. There was a widespread fear of the courts by defendants, and normally just the threat of court proceedings would be enough to force compliance, but in this case three of the defendants appear to have had a reasonable defence. In the end, however, it almost certainly had some effect in wearing them down.

Even during Thomas Atkinson's time, there may well have been a chronic problem with dwindling tithe income, and Lord Craven may have tried to remedy this by allowing the vicars to receive the tithe in hay, normally taken by him as impropriator.

This was however almost certainly before the Commonwealth, during which time tithes had become a hot political issue. Since then, what with inflation, much further erosion in the value of the customary fees had taken place. Both because of this and resentment against payment, it was becoming common for clergy to bring suits in the Church courts for 'subtraction' or withholding of tithes. In Wiltshire, for instance, during this period more than half its parishes experienced an action brought by the incumbent in the courts, while many more were settled out of court before litigation ever commenced.[73]

Thomas Dineley's view of Ludlow parish church, as it appeared in 1684. The St. John's chancel was fitted out for use as the bishop's court, and it was here that the case against Foulkes was heard over a period of almost two years. The building on the outside is little changed from its appearance today, except for a porch over the north door into the churchyard.

As we have seen, even Bishop Croft was bringing actions in his own court. Foulkes therefore was very far from being unusual in going to law, and he too was evidently attempting to remedy this dwindling in the value of his receipts, and in so doing was as much protecting his successors' income as his own. His robust stance on tithes is evident right from the beginning, when soon after his arrival in the parish he was actively pursuing some tithes unpaid from 1659, even before the time of his induction.[74]

In 1668, not long after his brush with Elizabeth Atkinson, but six years before any public knowledge of his involvement with Ann, he had sued a Thomas Moore, claiming payment for twenty acres of herbage or grazing on land in Stanton Lacy.

Moore's neighbouring landowner just happened to be Thomas Powys of Henley near Ludlow, an eminent Sergeant-at-Law, who took up Moore's cause, pointing out that a customary annual payment of nine shillings had long been acceptable to Foulkes' predecessors. Doubtless sensing when to leave well alone, in this instance Foulkes had backed down, personally visiting Powys at Henley to assure him that he had 'surceased his suit, And would give Moore noe further trouble'![75]

Relating to matters of tithe, Foulkes was also presented before the court for 'keeping a Terrier of the Gleab Lands, Gardens, Orchards, and Teyths to his owne private use', although in response to this he simply argued that all he had was the copy of the terrier (a schedule of the lands) and some record books kept by his predecessors. The presumption here appears to have been that only one copy of the terrier was permitted, and that should have been kept in the hands of the churchwardens. This allegation was however dismissed.[76]

The third and fourth articles of accusation were those that addressed the real substance of the case against Foulkes, and although they seem to be peppered with a mixture of hearsay anecdote, exaggeration, and rumour, some of which later vanishes from subsequent testimony, there was also substantial first-hand witness evidence.

Between 1673 and 1676, Foulkes was said to have 'frequented the company and society of severall loose, idle, and incontinent persons of the female sex, att unseasonable and unfitt houres, and in suspected places both by day and night', behaving himself 'very ymodestly, rudely, and undecently with them in kissinge, embraseinge, and wantonly dallyeinge and playeinge with them' on his lap or knee, but 'more particularly with one Anne Atkinson of the parish of Stanton Lacy'. There was also the 'common voyce, fame, and report' within the parish, and other parishes adjacent, that Foulkes had committed the 'foule synne of adultery or fornicacion' with Ann, 'and hath begott severall children, or at least one child on the body of the said Anne', and that as much had been admitted by Ann and Foulkes to members of her family. Suggesting that Foulkes might have had 'severall' children, and then retreating to the firmer ground of at least one, was perhaps a device as much for the benefit of courtroom effect as for keeping all options open, and was often repeated in the documents, although later there is evidence that there were indeed other pregnancies that did not come to term.

William Hopton testified that he had seen Foulkes both by night and day at the alehouse of the widow Partridge, on the Oldfield at Bromfield, where he had gone to drink and play bowls. Here he was observed kissing and embracing the landlady's daughter Ann, who was apparently 'of a scandalous reputation and loose behaviour'.[77]

Mary Withers had also witnessed Foulkes' growing lack of inhibition, at a time when she was still a member of Elizabeth's household. She, like Martha Dovey, had seen quite blatant improprieties at Hammond's farm, and Foulkes and Ann had appeared uninhibited even when under Elizabeth's nose. Mary claimed that she had 'severall times ... seen [Foulkes] goe into Ann's bedchamber, and there stay with her for some time, and when the mother of Ann hath been in bedd, Robert and Ann have gone together privately both within and without the house and continued each with other by night alone'.

She also saw Foulkes 'diverse times kiss and embrace Ann, playing and sporting very familiarly with her and thrusting his hands under her coats, and lifting them upp with his staff above her knees, and laing his hand upon her belly, and asking what shee had there and for whom she kept it, and useing diverse undecent and immodest expressions'.

Even when Ann had been in bed, Mary had known him to 'goe unto her and thrust his hand into the bedd and there stay and continue with her, kissing and wantonly embraceing and dallying with her'.[78]

Margaret Chearme, living in part of the same house, could not help seeing the couple over Christmas in 1675 'come out of the parlour, and in the hall [Robert] sat on a bench and called Ann to him, and took her betwixt his legs and clasped his arms about her middle, and hers about his neck, and [they] laid their faces togeather' for about a quarter of an hour. A day or two later, on New Years Eve, Grace Humphreys, a Welsh servant of the Chearme's, again saw them alone in the hall 'without any Candle but a small fire in the said room', Foulkes 'embraceing Ann with his Armes about her middle, and holding their faces close to each other'.[79]

One rather curious allegation was that Foulkes was also said to have called in three times on a certain Katharine Collins, who with her husband William occupied a cottage in Stanton Lacy, in the Green Lane. According to the story, while her husband was out, Foulkes had tried to tempt her to have sex with him but she refused, saying that this would imperil her soul and his too, at which Foulkes had said that she was a fool for thinking so, and as a minister he had the power to save her soul at any time in return for a payment of twopence.[80]

When Richard Chearme asked Katharine whether this was true, she was evasive, and enquired who had told him, she later going round to Foulkes to report what had been said. Katharine was afterwards stated to have emphatically denied any truth in the story, swearing that William Hopton had offered her 'a considerable reward' to testify that it was.[81] Hopton was even said to have 'allured' her into having a physical relationship with himself, and at the time of her denial

Katharine was heavily pregnant. If born alive, no resulting child was ever shown as baptized in the parish register.[82]

There are also a couple of anecdotes to show that Foulkes, in confident mood or in a rash unguarded moment, would on occasion let his tongue get the better of him. It was alleged that Ann had received several proposals of marriage from various suitors, Thomas Lloyd of Whittington Castle presumably being one, and that Foulkes had 'severall tymes or att least once... on purpose to hinder her marriage, in a vaunteinge manner declared and said, Lett whome will, have her or marry her... I am sure hee shall have none of her maydenhead, for she is a good natured girle and will water a mans nagg for him'! His hearers plainly took this as a flagrant boast that he and Ann were already well acquainted.[83]

It was Richard Chearme, the churchwarden, who claimed to have witnessed another outburst when Foulkes informed him, in the hall of the vicarage, that the Hoptons were nothing but a 'parcell of rogues and knaves'. Chearme reminded Foulkes that the Hoptons had powerful friends, and that 'they were acquainted with and befriended by' Sir Timothy Baldwyn, the bishop's chancellor, 'and he doubted not but with the Lord Bishopp and with most of the best gentlemen in the countrey'. Foulkes rashly retorted that he 'cared not a fart of his arse for the Lord Bishopp, nor the Chancellor, nor for any one of them all'![84] Despite Foulkes' later assurances of respect for his superiors, this declaration was to return to haunt him.

Much is also made of Foulkes' cruelty to Isabella. The effects of this, as we have already seen, were witnessed on at least one occasion by others, and she was said to have been the subject of abuse for at least several weeks. William Hopton reported Isabella telling him that Foulkes had even attempted 'to stabb her with a penknife and to strangle her with his handkercheafe whilst she lay in bedd with him'. So frightened was she for her life, believing that Foulkes was trying to poison her, that she felt compelled to send elsewhere for milk and other supplies in case he had tampered with what was in the house. Hopton claimed that Isabella had spoken to him of this, and had sent to his house for 'milke and drinke and other necessaries'. Foulkes dubiously countered that this was impossible because, at this particular time, Hopton did not yet have a house of his own, but he did not deny that Isabella believed herself to be under threat.

He was also said to have withdrawn himself from her bed 'for severall monthes or att least weekes togeather', either ejecting her from his bed, or sleeping in a room remote from her so that he 'might have the greater opportunity' to meet up with Ann. Isabella was not surprisingly intensely jealous, and quite naturally fought to save her marriage. She complained to Martha Dovey that her husband 'would never leave Anns company, and that Ann had stole his heart away from her'. She was also bitterly resentful of the fact that Foulkes' income was going to support the illegitimate child, and said that 'she could not endure it longer or conceave that the Revenues of the church should goe to maintaine that whore'.[85]

Foulkes otherwise refrained from commenting about his domestic relationship with Isabella, other than relying on witnesses to testify that normally they had been very affectionate with one another, he calling her 'Nibby', Sweetheart, and other terms of endearment. The powers of a woman over her husband were at this time very limited, and the only check upon his unreasonable behaviour was public opinion, and his reputation within the family and community. This was an age moreover when it was not considered unreasonable for a husband to chastise his wife for wrongdoing. On the other hand, the ideal advocated by the

Church was a loving, forgiving, and respectful relationship, and the clergy in particular were expected to give an example to their flock.

The status of a clergyman, nevertheless, gave him even more authority over his wife, and it was at the time of their falling out that Foulkes denied Isabella the sacrament, using his power as parish priest to withhold from her the solace of taking communion. He was said to have deliberately picked a quarrel with her 'without any lawfull cause, and on purpose to disturb her in the preparation for receiving' the sacrament, and threatened that if she came forward to the altar he would 'reject her and turn her back with shame'. This had caused her great grief and sorrow of heart, and this she told to several people in the parish. Foulkes later explained that his wife at this time was in no 'condition' to take communion and, according to the rubric of the Book of Common Prayer, to prevent her was technically well within his authority. It does nonetheless sound suspiciously as if he had indeed used this to coerce her into being acquiescent while he indulged himself with Ann, and it does not reflect well on him.

The rubric states, firstly, that the curate was not to allow any 'open and notorious evil liver', or one who had done wrong to his neighbours in word or deed, to partake of the sacrament unless he had openly declared himself penitent. Similarly, two or more people between whom there was 'malice and hatred' were prohibited until they were reconciled, although any one of them repenting could be readmitted. It was also widely believed among the laity at this time that if any persons took communion in an unfit state, then it would put their souls at risk of being damned.

This was not helped by the wording of the exhortation read out by the priest on the Sunday or holy day before communion was to be taken. The congregation was warned that those that were unrepentant, did not promise to amend their ways, or were unreconciled with their enemies, did nothing else but increase their damnation by receiving the sacrament. It followed that taking communion from a priest towards whom a communicant felt hostile would also put the receiver at risk, and of course this may well have applied to Isabella Foulkes.

But then, if the priest himself was the 'notorious evil liver', might not even the sacrament itself be valueless, or worse? Not according to the 26th Article of Religion, which maintained that '... neither is the effect of Christ's ordinance taken away by their wickedness, nor the grace of God's gifts diminished from such as by faith and rightly do receive the Sacraments ministered unto them... *although they be ministered by evil men*'.

So, despite all this, attendance was still compulsory at the parish church; and so we can understand the appearance of William and Mary Hopton in the consistory court in December 1676, when they were presented for 'not frequenting the parish church of Staunton Lacy, and refuseing to hear Mr Robert Foulkes the present vicar there preach, but goeing to Culmington church or other adjacent churches on Sundayes to hear divine service and sermons, declaring the reason of their soe doeing is... they cannott edifie by the doctrine of the said Mr Foulkes, in regard he doth give them very evill examples by his own ungodly, irreligious, and unchaste life and conversation'.[86]

What is not mentioned, considering Hopton's pivotal role in the harassment of his vicar, is whether Foulkes had actually turned the couple away from receiving the sacrament at his hands, although one of Hopton's justifications for not attending his church was that 'Mr Foulkes did tell and threaten [him] that he was damned'. In the circumstances of the open conflict, therefore, partaking of communion there would surely have been almost impossible.

In spite of this, in 1677 William Hopton was once again presented before the court 'for not duely comeing to his own parish church, and for not receving the holy Sacrament there at Easter last'.[87] Easter, Whitsuntide, and Christmas were the major festivals in the year when all parishioners were expected to take communion, even though they risked being denied it and thereby publicly shamed by their parish priest. So here at least, it seems, Hopton may have found himself between a rock and a hard place. It is notable, however, that all Foulkes' other accusers appear to have attended the parish church as usual.

That parishioners did indeed withdraw from taking communion, if they felt their salvation endangered by doing so, was not that unusual an event. A particularly well-documented instance had taken place in the Wiltshire parish of Somerford Magna in 1673, when a group of thirteen parishioners petitioned the Bishop of Salisbury for support against their rector, the Revd. Nathaniel Aske.[88] Aske was a troubled spirit, a contentious, confrontational, and litigious man, who so alienated his congregation with his consistently aggressive behaviour that they stayed away from his church.

Consequently he presented them in the consistory court for this and, most seriously of all, for failing to take communion at the previous Easter and Whitsunday. Their defence was that they could not with a good conscience receive the sacrament from his hands although, they said, they longed to receive it. Much to the fury of the rector, the bishop's registrar treated the petitioners with extreme leniency, dismissing all charges against them and remitting their court fees, but warning them to take communion at the next Christmas. Despite this, the rector brought yet further court actions whenever opportunities arose, and the situation was only finally resolved by the appointment of a curate, followed by Aske's death just over two years later.

OF EYES AND EARS

'Robert walked hastily fromwards his owne house, though it was near and from the Town, alsoe by a private or by way into the fields, diverse people following him, clapping their hands, and hooting at him ...'

Foulkes and Ann were now the subjects of close surveillance, and every move they made was being observed in the hope it might provide further evidence for the court proceedings.[89] Watchers were not disappointed. William Hopton testified that even after the bishop's admonition he had several times seen Foulkes and Ann 'togeather alone, hand in hand, very familiarly in private places, as in meadows or leasowes through which there was noe common or publick way, and there they have continued about the space of a Quarter of an hower', and were still there after he had gone. Chearme, living in part of the same house as Ann, saw Foulkes there on a number of occasions, and could hear them talking together behind a closed door.

On one particularly memorable occasion, Hopton and Chearme were told that Foulkes and Ann were keeping a tryst at the house of Francis Underwood in Stanton Lacy, to which they had gone 'by private and unusuall wayes', hoping to get together without raising suspicion. Underwood, it seems, was Ann's tenant and so had little say in the matter, in fact it was suggested that because of this he dared not interfere. To confirm the truth of their information, Hopton and Chearme now called at the house on the pretext of collecting Underwood's church dues; and on seeing his wife, Judith, they enquired whether Foulkes was there, only to be told that her husband was away, and that only she and her daughter were at home. They then asked her bluntly whether Foulkes and Ann were there together, which she denied, after which they now searched the house 'below stairs'. Here they found only a locked door to a 'little private room', and calling out to Foulkes asked him whether he remembered the bishop's admonition, 'and whether he were not ashamed to be there in company with a whore, and bidd him for shame goe home to his wife', to which not surprisingly there came no reply.

They then withdrew but kept further watch, and after about half an hour they saw Foulkes come out and walk hurriedly away, Ann coming with him as far as the door, but stepping back when she saw that they were observed.

Hopton called out to Foulkes, 'and asked him againe if he were not ashamed to keep company with a whore', to which Foulkes retorted 'Be hanged, you Rogue!' and hurried off through the fields, in a direction away from his own house and the village, 'diverse people following him, clapping their hands, and hooting at him'![90]

Those on watch, meanwhile, continued their vigil around the house, and saw Ann come several times to a window, peeping out to see whether the coast was clear. Later, after about two and a half hours, Underwood's wife went and fetched Elizabeth Atkinson, who after a further half hour sent Francis Underwood off to drink at the alehouse to draw Hopton away. This ruse did not work, and only after darkness had fallen did Ann, Elizabeth, and Judith Underwood feel safe enough to leave the house together, taking a route through a private orchard to return home. Hopton also claimed that there had been several other assignations in the same place. He had seen drink being carried there by Underwood or his daughter Elizabeth, and knew of trysts lasting four to five hours, and then of Foulkes and Ann being seen to leave the house, one after the other.[91]

Not only tenants but also servants could find themselves caught up in the crossfire between factions, and therefore liable to interrogation and pressure. Foulkes placed his manservant, John Boland, on several occasions at Ann's disposal, and she was seen being carried behind him to Ludlow on Foulkes' horse. On the other hand, servants must also have been a common source of leakage when it came to family confidences, and not all domestic employees were so loyal or compliant as Boland or Underwood. In fact eyes and ears were just as likely to have been placed below stairs. In Foulkes' household this was the maidservant, Joan Wood, who was later said by him to have been 'intimately or rather impudently acquainted with... William Hopton, and was usually, after Mr Foulkes and his wife were gonn to bedd, to goe to the house of the said Hopton and there to debauch herself and drinke with him ... and other rude and vicious persons. And Mr Foulkes turned her out of his service, and the rather because the said Woode had a sister who was famed to be incontinent with the said William Hopton, soe that Joane Woode came through mallice and revenge to give her testimony in this pretended business thinginge thereby to do Mr Foulkes a prejudice'.

While there can be little doubt that Joan Wood must have been an invaluable source of gossip and information for Hopton, she was only in Foulkes' employ for about seven weeks, during June and July of 1676; and it was she who had raised the alarm when Foulkes had assaulted Isabella.[92] Though not mentioned in her deposition, Joan may well be the unnamed maidservant whom Foulkes was reputed to have molested. A prosecution question was directed at a Mr. John Goodwyn, who was asked whether he had not seen Foulkes, in his presence, 'behave himselfe most rudely and immodestly towardes his owne servant maide, and in his owne house'. Goodwyn was asked whether Foulkes had not 'used soe much incivility towards his owne servant maide in the night season that hee had made her squeake and cry out, and was not the candle thereupon putt out, and did not the maide complayne of the rudeness of her master?'.

Although Goodwyn's response was not preserved, we shall see from evidence given later that Foulkes was not averse on occasion, when the opportunity presented itself, to being 'playful' with female servants, even those not his own. It was,

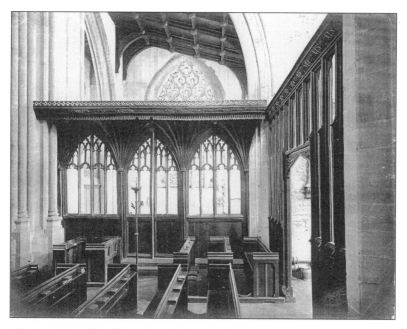

The interior of Ludlow parish church, showing the screen of the Lady Chapel. In Foulkes' day this was used as the Corporation chapel, and Archdeacon's chancel. On the right is St. Catherine's chancel, formerly the guild chapel of the Weavers. From a photograph by Walter Harper, taken in about 1929.

on the other hand, by no means unusual for such girls to be at risk in the wealthier households of the time, if not from the attentions of their master then from his sons.

OF HIS PARISH DUTIES

'That you Robert Foulkes, beinge vicar of the parish church of Staunton Lacy, and haveing taken upon you the Cure and Care of your parishioners soules, ought to use your best endeavour to instruct them in the way of Religion and holynesse of life, and not to neglect or omitt any opportunity or place whereby or wherein you might further the salvacion of their soules, yet notwithstandinge you have severall tymes within theise three yeares last past wholly neglected your duty as minister of the parish Church of Staunton Lacy ...'

To compound the trouble that he was in with the Church authorities, several allegations were now levelled at Foulkes suggesting that he had neglected his parochial responsibilities. In August 1676, Richard Chearme had presented him before the consistory court for 'neglectinge his duty and absentinge himselfe from the Church, and leaveinge it destitute of divine service for some Sundayes within this yeare last past, and for neglectinge to instruct the youth in the Church Caterchisme for theise two yeares last past'. On top of this it was said he had omitted to read divine service on holy days, fasting days, and Ember weeks; refused to visit the sick and to administer the sacrament 'although desired in the extreamity of sickness'; and he had failed to go on the perambulation to beat the parish bounds during Rogation week.[93] It was once even hinted that he had 'pretended' to go to preach at other churches, leaving his own without a preacher, although this was never enlarged upon, nor proof of him having done so ever put forward.

Elizabeth Atkinson, in Foulkes' defence, responded that he 'being ... sick in body and advised by his Physicians not to goe abroad, did leave his Church without service or sermon upon one Lords day in the morning, but hath constantly either served the Cure himselfe or provided another fitt person to supply and serve the said Cure in his absence'. She added that upon 'some Sundays and holydays in the winter time ... Mr. Foulks hath not chatechized the youth of the parish, and upon some Wednesdays and Fridays hath not read the Letany in the said Church; but for the greatest part of the year he hath chatechised and read the Letany, and hath duely and carefully served his Cure'.[94] John Slade, then vicar at the neighbouring church of Bromfield two miles away, said that he had on several occasions assisted Foulkes by reading divine service and preaching at Stanton Lacy, and added that Foulkes 'always seemed carefull to have his Cure supplied in his absence'.[95]

Foulkes, in his own defence, commented that he had always done his best to fulfil his duties according to the 'rubrick and liturgy of the Church of England', and that he had 'duely instructed and examined the children and youth of his parish in the church caterchism, now by law set forthe and appoynted upon Sundayes, except when the parishoners omitted or neglected to send theyre Children'. He added that 'in all other his ministeriall offices and duties', he was 'carefull, painefull, observant, and pious ... accordinge to the lawes statutes and cannons of the Church of England'. Considering all the evidence, on balance he does appear to have been a conscientious parish priest.

OF FEVER, AND A FUNERAL

Although apparently not noted in local parish burial registers, some of the statements refer to an outbreak of a fever in the Ludlow neighbourhood. Richard Hopton the younger claimed that in May 1676 he was drinking with Foulkes and others in an alehouse, when the vicar was asked by the servant of a John Brompton of the Stocking to visit, with all possible speed, his master who lay very sick and weak.

Foulkes, who was himself then recovering from serious illness, had refused to go, and Brompton had died on the following day. Visitation of the very sick and terminally ill was an important duty of parish priests, but Foulkes maintained that this was at the time when he was 'very ill himselfe and weake in body, and was not able to goe to him, and the person who desired his visitacion was sicke of a pestilential distemper, and his owne relacions were afrayed of comeinge neare him'. Indeed, a priest might justifiably be excused from visiting if the illness was plague, or considered contagious.

It was nevertheless while sickening at the start of this serious illness, later leaving him weak and unable to work, that Foulkes had attended the nearby funeral of a 'special friend'.

Hopton testified that on the day before Easter in 1676, being a day on which parishioners were used to receiving the sacrament, they had turned up at the church that morning 'expecting to hear prayers there read and the sacrament (accordinge to custom) administered, and staid there about an hower or two looking for Mr Foulks, and then sent the parish clark to the said Mr Foulks house to know the reason for his absence'. Foulkes told the clerk that he was sick and unable to attend at the church, and asked that the parishioners should return to their homes.

Some then went to Hopton's house and complained of their disappointment; but not long afterwards that morning Hopton saw Foulkes ride out from his house, and later met him at the funeral of a Richard Herbert at Bromfield, where he 'there saw him and heard him discourse and talke heartily without any shew or sign of any sickness or distemper'.[96]

Chearme's simpler version of these events was that Foulkes, 'being somewhat sick and indisposed in body did goe from home unto the funerall of Richard Herbert Esquire at Bromfield about 9 or 10 o'clock in the morning, and neglected to administer the... sacrament or to read prayers in his church, although diverse of the parishioners came thither expecting the same, and prepared to receive the said sacrament and to hear divine service there to be read, but were wholy disappointed.'

In Foulkes' defence, Ann's brother John said that he had later met him coming back from Bromfield, and that Foulkes had complained to him 'that he was sick and not able to stay at the funerall, and [Atkinson] being a practitioner in physick told [Foulkes] that he thought him madd, and that he had a minde to be in Mr Herberts condicion, and advised him to hasten home and keepe himself warm; and that very night [Foulkes] fell desperately ill of the feaver, much of the same nature with that of which Mr Herbert dyed, and [Atkinson] was sent to him in hast that night, and other practitioners in physick, with chirurgians and apothecaryes afterwards, and he labourd under that distemper above a moneth after that time, not able to supply his cure without danger of his life.' Elizabeth Atkinson confirmed that Foulkes felt so unwell at the funeral that he was forced to come away before the burial, and added that when he 'came home he was soe extreamly sick that [she] thought he would have dyed, and fainting soe often that [she] was forced to rubb his temples with strong waters, and then sent for physitians to him'.[97]

During his convalescence, there were those who may, rather uncharitably, have thought that he had prolonged a little his need to take things easy, and Hopton suggested that latterly he was actually 'pretending' himself still sick. He remarked that Foulkes had been advised that he 'could drink nothing but what was warme', yet Foulkes came to Hopton's alehouse, 'and there being a letter then brought unto him from one Mr Brampton which pleased him, he took up a glass full of cold Ale and drank it all off as the said Mr Brampton's health, and continued drinking cold ale for most part of the night.'. Nevertheless, there seems little doubt that for some weeks at least the vicar was seriously ill; and for Foulkes, it was this time of crisis that almost caused him to turn away from his 'beloved sin'. Indeed it was to this period that he later referred, during his last days in Newgate prison, when he ruefully remembered his feelings while contemplating what seemed his likely death from the fever:

Once [my own Conscience] charged me very furiously; and having the advantage of a great fit of sickness, it made such assaults upon me, that sin had like to have lost its hold, for I was driven into great fears, and deep apprehensions, (Oh that I had still continued such a Convert!) those fears extorted confessions, the confessions begat vows and promises; but woe is me, they all proved abortive, for I soon returned to my vomit, and the health of my body renewed the disease of my soul; the tyrant Sin soon recovers its dominion, and ever since Conscience has been kept under hatches.[98]

Opposite: A near-by church interior of Foulkes' time, and one that he would probably have known well. The nave of Stokesay parish church was rebuilt during, and just after, the Commonweath, following extensive Civil War damage and fire. From a photograph taken by W. A. Call of Monmouth.

CHAPTER 7

Friends and Favourers

'And to palliate and hide my sin the more, I studied to be more elaborate and zealous in my Preaching, to the great satisfaction of my Hearers; only I seldom medled with, or but very tenderly touched my own beloved sin. I went about all the parts of my Ministerial duty so carefully, and discharged them with such approbation, that the judgements of many charitable and well-meaning persons not only acquitted me of the vices I stood charged with, but I deluded their good opinion into some thoughts of my innocency and virtue.'

To counter the long list of accusations, there were several groups of witnesses who now gave evidence in Foulkes' defence. Whether they sprang to do so is debatable, for it cannot have been anything but a tedious grind to be embroiled in the machinery of the court. This was however the 17th-century, when there were many who were ever ready to go to litigation, and indeed there appear to have been some who were practically addicted to it. A few will have enjoyed their moment of importance, while others, depite their assurances that they came to bear witness freely, will have felt that they had been cajoled, obligated, or possibly even coerced, into giving evidence for either side.

We know that Foulkes went out of his way to indulge his allies for, as we shall see, he admitted that he had spent time and money in treating "friends and favourers" of his cause. For many though, particularly of advancing years, it was doubtless a wearying experience, and some will have been bitterly sickened that the whole situation had been allowed to develop in the first place.

The first to defend Foulkes were the Atkinson family, who rallied round primarily to shield Ann. Of course, if Foulkes fell then so did she, so the two had to be defended together, whatever the family's opinion might be of the whole silly affair. They clearly knew much more than they were admitting, indeed they were generally very 'economical with the truth', when not actually dissembling or lying through their teeth. Their evidence was very much in agreement and carefully worded, although on occasion under cross-questioning some revealing admissions slipped through.

Their testimony generally agreed that 'on their consciences' they did not believe that Foulkes and Ann had been intimate together because they had never actually seen any 'uncivill or dishonest accion between them'; or when questioned about their affair, Foulkes and Ann 'with horrid excracions' had always vehemently denied its existence.

For two years Ann had been away from Stanton Lacy in London and elsewhere, and Foulkes had remained at his post, so nothing possibly could have happened during that time.

They were all convinced that the stories about the affair had originated with the Hoptons, who were motivated out of malice and revenge, and that there was a conspiracy to deprive Foulkes of his living. Yes, they had heard that Foulkes had quarrelled with and beaten his wife, but in their experience he and Isabella were otherwise always very loving and affectionate with one another, he calling her 'Nibby', and other terms of endearment.

Elizabeth Atkinson recalled that about three years before, Richard Hopton the elder 'labouring under some distemper of body and insanity of mind' did say that Ann had had a child, but that on 'examination' he had then denied it. She had later confronted Richard Hopton junior with this, and he had told and confessed to her that he knew nothing of it but had 'heard it from one Symonds of Shrewsbury since dead'. Of course Hopton knew that this could never have been checked up on, but for Elizabeth to quote Hopton's own denial in the face of his accusation was a compelling riposte.

She also explained how the Foulkes and Atkinson families were intimately acquainted, because Isabella had been 'educated' by her, and so Foulkes and his wife were often in Elizabeth's house. Foulkes never kissed Ann unless she had returned after being away, or 'he might salute her by way of courtesie and noe otherwise'. Elizabeth had heard that a child had been born, but believed 'in her conscience that [Ann was] a spotless maid, for that Ann hath often with weeping eyes and bitter protestations told [Elizabeth] that she knew not [Foulkes] nor any other man more than by their outward habitts'.

Elizabeth was also emphatic that Foulkes spoke of the bishop and his chancellor 'with great esteem and reverence', and that he had observed the bishop's admonition. If he had failed to read the Litany on Wednesdays and Fridays, then this was 'not out of any neglect of his office, but in regard almost none of his parishioners would come to church to hear him upon those days'. Elizabeth did however admit, on being questioned, that Isabella had complained to her that she had received a beating.

There were more stories about William Hopton. He had jested in the churchyard that he would send his illegitimate son 'to school for some time in the countrey, and then would send him to the lord bishop of Hereford to make a parson of', or that he would marry him off to Ann's daughter. Hopton quipped to Chearme that he was sure that his son would make as good a parson as a certain Jerry Bayton, whom it appears had lately been ordained by Bishop Croft, although whether this was a hint that Bayton was also illegitimate is unclear. Later, Foulkes dismissively remarked that he was merely a 'vaine and idle fellow of a lay profession'.

There was also Margaret, a former servant to Mr. Richard Gravenor of Whitbach, who had told Elizabeth that a relative of hers had met Hopton on the road and that he had offered her half a crown to have sex with him. After refusing to get up behind him on his horse, she resisted him, and he had 'Layd violent handes upon her, and by his force and rudeness tore some of her Cloathes...'

The Reverend Francis Atkinson's statement, despite his involvement in baptizing the child at West Felton, and arranging for funds to maintain her, is remarkable only for its reticence. His active participation in this whole business must have been a considerable embarrassment; and not unnaturally, fearing that it could have implications for his own career, he chose to remain tight-lipped.

In court he simply denied any knowledge of the affair, but testified that he had often seen Foulkes and Ann walking together, but always as neighbours, and that they had never avoided his company; nor had he seen them being familiar together in suspicious circumstances. He therefore believed that the rumour that they had had an illegitimate child was 'fraudulous and false' because, he said, 'neither Robert Foulkes nor Ann, being [his] sister, did ever confess to [him] of any such crime'!

Atkinson was also part of another group, Foulkes' fellow clergy, who now stood witness in his defence. The evidence of John Slade, vicar of Bromfield, as we have already heard, testified how Foulkes had always appeared careful to cover his absences. He also described his encounter with Foulkes at the widow Partridge's alehouse on Old Field, telling him of his concern about the rumours circulating about him and Ann, and requesting that they should avoid each other's company. He added that Foulkes, at the time, had taken this advice 'very kindly and quietly'.

Dr. William Bradley, rector of West Felton, was the most distant from Foulkes' own parish, but was able to testify about his conversation when William Hopton had called in on him in June 1676, and clearly Hopton had not made a good impression. Francis Atkinson had been Bradley's curate for about seven years, during which time he had lived at the parsonage house, but ate his meals out at a Mr. Rogers' house nearby; and Ann had been with him about four years ago to his best remembrance. Bradley also remarked that he had first met Foulkes in about 1669 at a public meeting in Shrewsbury, but did not believe the rumours about Foulkes and Ann, 'for that he never saw anything from either of them or their carriage but what was modest and very civill'.[99]

Perhaps the most influential of the local clerical witnesses was Ralph Fenton, then rector of Ludlow for some 18 years. He was some seven years older than Foulkes, and had followed a similar career in that he had matriculated at Oxford but was not a graduate. He had been installed as rector in about 1658 during the interregnum, and in addition had been appointed town Preacher in 1661. Fenton's role as defence witness must have been somewhat complicated by the fact that he was also acting as the chancellor's deputy during the court proceedings, including the day on which he gave evidence. The documents show that he presided over a number of sessions during the hearings of Foulkes' case, and many of the witnesses' depositions were heard and signed by him.[100]

Although it seems very likely that Fenton either knew or at least suspected more than he was acknowledging, he must have seen his prime function as trying to maintain the dignity and credibility of the local clergy, and thus to limit the damage caused by this whole sorry affair.

His evidence was therefore somewhat carefully worded.[101] He testified to having known Foulkes throughout his time at Stanton Lacy, and had 'observed his carriage and behaveour, and always found it sober, and honest, and loveing, and friendly, and peaceable'; and said that he conducted himself in public 'very modestly, decently, and piously becoming his calling'. He had also heard several of Foulkes' parishioners and others commend their vicar for his 'diligence and industry' in performing his ministerial duties.

The rector had first heard the story of the illegitimate baby from Richard Hopton senior, who had said that the child had been taken from West Felton to nurse near Bridgnorth, and that Hopton 'had acquainted [Ann's] uncle Mr Whitmore therewith, and thereupon the child was presently removed hence'. Nowhere else does this Bridgnorth version of the story appear in the evidence, although John Atkinson did mention that Ann stayed for a time with her uncle at 'Ludson'.[102] Fenton believed however that Hopton's story was spoken maliciously, and with intent to disgrace and defame Ann and Foulkes, because 'he uttered those words with exceeding much passion and violence, and in a clamorous manner'.

He also heard that William Hopton had 'scattered and spread abroad' the story 'by makeing it his business in all places and companies to discourse of it publicly and privately, by endeavouring to bespatter and lessen the creditt and good repute' of Foulkes. Fenton had also taken 'more than ordinary notice of the kind and affectionate carriage of [Foulkes] and his wife each to other', and that Foulkes always seemed a kind and loving husband. He did nonetheless admit, under further probing, that he had been approached by Isabella who did 'severall times complaine of [Foulkes], and of his keeping Ann Atkinson company, and of his unkindness to his wife thereupon'.

Next to testify on Foulkes' behalf were two lawyers. One was Edward Smalman who, as we shall see in the next chapter, was able to give evidence about William Hopton's misappropriation of legal documents.

The other lawyer was William Hall of Barnard's Inn, born in Cardington, and a counsellor in the King's Bench court, who described how he had been in company with Hopton in September 1676, at the house of a Richard Condy in Ludlow, now dead; and that Hall had mentioned that he had brought down a writ on Foulkes' behalf, that concerned a Thomas Jones of Stanton Lacy and an agreement about tithes. Hopton tried to persuade Hall to let him have the writ so that 'he would break it up at his own chardg'. Although told that there had already been a settlement, Hopton continued to press him to let him have the writ, leaving Hall convinced that he intended 'to doe [Foulkes] a prejudice'.[103]

Lastly, among Foulkes' defenders, were his own parishioners, who at least seem to have borne out Ralph

Fenton's opinion that Foulkes was conscientious in his duties, and well respected. Many had known Foulkes for years, and said that that he was 'very kind and charitable' to them, and that he had only ever failed in his duties when illness prevented him. Several, as we have heard, also testified that he had resolved disputes between them and their neighbours, and that he was not a contentious man.

Admittedly, once litigation was in full swing, Foulkes had worked hard to influence people to testify in his defence, for he later wrote in his confession that he 'had suits depending both in the Civil and Ecclesiastical Courts; and to support the credit and Interest of the Causes, I spent I confess, too much of my time, too much of my Money in publick Houses, to treat the friends and favourers of the Suits, especially those whose interest it was to promote and continue them; there I staid long, and drank to intemperance'.[104] Those who testified in his defence, nevertheless, do appear genuinely to have liked and respected him; and whether Foulkes had actually, as he maintained, 'deluded' them into defending him, is perhaps not entirely true.

During his defence, Foulkes had also made much, throughout the eighteen month or so duration of the proceedings, of the 'combination' between his accusers, implying a malicious conspiracy to which the parties were bound by money. Amongst the court papers preserved at the Herefordshire Record Office is a loose undated note, written in Robert Foulkes' distinctive hand, and passed by him to the Registrar during the proceedings. It reads:[105]

Mr. Register
I desire that Margarett Chearme may be examined Whether she knowes or beleeves that there is any Contract or Combinacion betweene Richard Hopton, William Hopton, Joseph Dovy, & Richard Chearme, to hold togeather in the prosecucion

of this Matter, and whether she knowes or beleeves Whether that Hutchison the promotor does It of his owne Accord or by theyre instigacion, At his owne charge or theyre contribucion, & whether H[utchison] doe it out of Conscience or Mallice

pray fayle not
your Servant R. Foulkes

Here Foulkes was plainly hoping to discredit the action as a plot to bring him down, motivated merely out of malice, and perhaps there is also just a hint here of paranoia. His accusers responded quite reasonably that they had simply contributed to a common fund in order to share the burden of their legal fees, rather than one member bearing all the costs. This was an age in which litigation was said to have been

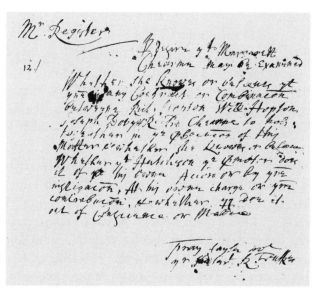

Robert Foulkes' hastily scrawled note, in his very distinctive hand, instructing the court registrar to question Margaret Chearme about the alleged conspiracy between the 'combinators', and about Hutchinson's motives in agreeing to act as promotor. The full transcript is opposite and above on pages 84-85. *(Reproduced by permission of the Diocese of Hereford)*

the most popular of contemporary pastimes, and the number of barristers per head of population peaked at around this time.[106] Lawyers have always been expensive, and one cannot see how else his accusers should have set about it, but Foulkes did his best to imply that this was evidence for corrupt dealing and conspiracy.

Whether this would have swayed the Court seems dubious, but Hutchinson was later very concerned to try to distance himself from the financial arrangements, saying that he was not the one who had actually retained their counsel, Richard Cornwall. Only on one occasion had he himself actually handled any money, and this was when he passed on fifty shillings, which had been given by Richard Chearme to Hopton, and then by him to Hutchinson, to be handed to their proctor.

Another plank in Foulkes' conspiracy theory, mentioned in his defence, was one in which Joseph and Martha Dovey were said to have attempted to put one of their children, 'supposed to be unlawfully begotten', out to nurse at Worcester.[107] The idea, allegedly, was that this should be done in Foulkes' name, in order to discredit him. Whether there was any substance to this story, or indeed whether it was ever established as being true, is never revealed, although a note in Foulkes' hand was passed to his lawyer in court, instructing him to question a certain Mr. Ballard about the matter.

Further doubts on the Doveys' probity were cast by the mentioning of Martha being 'suspected to have delivered one Briscoe (beinge a Daughter to her the said Martha) of a Childe in a private and Clandestine manner, which Childe was Concealed and Denyed and supposed to be buryed in a Garden, but afterwards suspected to be throwne into a house of office ...'. This matter had apparently been investigated by two Justices of the Peace and the Coroner, who came to

Stanton Lacy especially, upon the report that a baby had been born prematurely but dead, and 'noe bigger than a Rabbett'.[108]

A further note in Foulkes' handwriting is revealing in that it may give us an insight into his attitude towards Elizabeth Atkinson. Among the entries in the Court Book is one in which Foulkes was said to have uttered 'scandalous words against Elizabeth Atkinson ... calling her old whore, old Bawd, and Jezabell, and other such names'. William Hopton said that Foulkes had also called her 'a dissembling bich', and that 'she was able to undoe a whole Countrey', presumably implying that she could stir up trouble in the neighbourhood.[109]

For her part, Elizabeth throughout the case appears to have been stout in his and Ann's defence, and this must surely have been something of an ordeal for a woman of seventy in having to take the stand on at least three occasions and

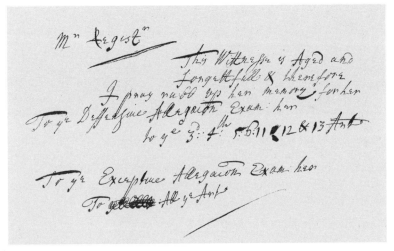

Another note in Foulkes' hand, addressed to the Registrar of the court. It reads:
'This Wittnesse is Aged and Forgetfull & therefore I pray rubb up her memory for her'. There are then instructions to question her on specific topics. *(Reproduced by permission of the Diocese of Hereford)*

be cross-examined in court. Foulkes' public attitude to her, nonetheless, does seem to have been somewhat condescending; and a second scrappy note, written in haste to the Registrar, reads: 'this wittnesse is aged and forgettfull, and therefore I pray rubb up her memory for her'! Elizabeth seems to be the only aged witness to whom these words could possibly refer.

Above: The Old Talbot Inn in Sidbury, Worcester, where Foulkes and Ann spent a night in late September 1674. It has greatly changed since then, although much of the original timber frame survives on the interior. Another building to the west was demolished to make way for recent road widening.

Opposite: The old Market Hall at Shrewsbury was built in 1595, and faces the site of the Three Tunns tavern where Ann Atkinson was found 'in company' during the Assizes in August 1677. From an engraving published in 1837.

CHAPTER 8

The Shrewsbury Assizes

'Item. That noe faith or Creditt is or ought to be given to the sayinges and deposicions of William Hopton, for that he is a person that... is under a Greate and stronge suspicion of Dishonest and fraudulent accions in severall thinges, and in particular for privily takinge a Packett of Records of Nisi prius from one Edward Miles, a carrier of Ludlow, for which he the said Hopton was Indicted by order of the Judge of the Assizes held for the County of Salop.'

The weakest link in the complainants' case against their vicar came not in their arguments about his conduct, but in the recklessly corrupt behaviour and greed of their most vociferous witness. This was almost to result in the complete undoing of the case against Foulkes.

89

It is already apparent that William Hopton, out of revenge and for personal gain, was quite prepared to have the terms of other people's leases revised without their knowledge. It also seems that he even thought little of personally amending signed and sealed documents when he thought it convenient. As an agent to Lord Craven he must have had frequent access to legal documents and therefore need to consult lawyers, one of whom was the Ludlow attorney, Edward Smalman, who lived at No. 55 Broad Street.

Smalman was one of the many lawyers making a lucrative living attending to the needs of the litigants in the courts in both church and castle, and some years later he was to become town clerk. A Ludlow ironmonger, Richard Davies, one day came to Smalman accompanied by one Faulkner, asking his advice about a lease which had been procured by Hopton from Lord Craven 'for the lives of him the said Faulkner, and his wife and child'. When told that the names of the wife and child were wrong, Hopton in Faulkner's presence had simply erased the original names and inserted the correct ones. Worried that the lease might no longer be valid, Faulkner was brought to Smalman who advised him that it must be returned to Lord Craven, the alterations noted, and the document sealed afresh.

Meanwhile Hopton's capacity for intrigue and skulduggery was to rise to yet greater heights, and Smalman was to find himself drawn ever more deeply into this story. As well as harbouring his own growing suspicions of Hopton's integrity, the lawyer was also to become involved in a suit against him, acting as attorney on behalf of Elizabeth Atkinson. In addition, Smalman was representing Ann Atkinson in a case to recover rent from Richard Hopton the elder; and also Foulkes, who was suing both William Hopton and Chearme.

Following a difference in opinion between Smalman and Samuel Brompton, the solicitor acting for the Hoptons and

Chearme, the lawyers agreed that an agent in the Court of Common Pleas should 'send down the Records in those 3 suites to have them tryed at [the] Lent Assizes for the County of Salop, and accordingly they were dispatched and delivered to Edward Miles, a carrier in Ludlow'.[110] Miles then came to Smalman to tell him that the packet, clearly addressed to the attorney, had indeed been brought by him to his warehouse, but that William Hopton had called in and taken it away. Furthermore, when confronted with this, Hopton had brazenly responded by offering to indemnify Miles against any claim made by the lawyers to a limit of one hundred pounds.

Smalman promptly complained to the assize judge, and obtained a warrant against Hopton for purloining the documents, 'who being thereupon apprehended and brought before the said Judge, he denied the haveing or seeing of them, and offered to take his oath that he never saw or had in his hands any such packett.' The judge, nonetheless, being well satisfied by ample evidence to the contrary, immediately had a bill of indictment drawn up against Hopton, and subsequently 'the same, upon full proofe made there upon the said bill, was found by the Grand Jury.'[111]

Although it is not clear from the records, it seems likely that the hearing of the '3 suites' at the Lent Assizes had been postponed as a result of the loss of the papers, the trial of Hopton being held at the Shrewsbury assizes in August 1677. It is also probable that the three other cases were heard at the same sitting since a party of inhabitants from Stanton Lacy and Ludlow travelled the thirty miles north to attend the court. This outing was to prove the perfect opportunity for yet more gossip and intrigue, and led to further accusations against Foulkes during the following month, it being alleged that he had quarrelled with his wife while at Shrewsbury, struck her, and then packed her off home with a neighbour, before taking the opportunity to spend a night with Ann. Fortunately for Foulkes several reliable witnesses around him were able to testify that this rumour was a gross exaggeration, although it was not entirely without foundation.

Isabella Foulkes had been called as a witness for the Crown, presumably to testify to Hopton's attempt to revise the terms of the Atkinson's leases. Ann was there too, as both plaintiff and witness; also her brother John, Foulkes himself, Edward Smalman, and several others. Somerset Wall, a yeoman and at that time a Stanton Lacy churchwarden, later gave evidence that he had met Foulkes and his wife at Shrewsbury on the 11th of August 'being in the Assize time, and walking along the street saw Ann Atkinson and her brother standing in the street, and [Foulkes] only spake to them as he passed by them.'

Next day, on the Saturday morning a little before dinner, Wall accompanied Foulkes 'unto his Inn at the sign of the Fox in Shrewsbury and there mett with [Foulkes'] wife who in [Wall's] apprehension had drank a little too much, and [Foulkes] takeing notice thereof was much troubled and complained of it to [Wall], and after dinner [Isabella] went out of the room wherein she dyned and [Foulkes] followed her', but where they had gone, or what happened next, he did not know.[112]

Later that day Wall was told that Foulkes had struck his wife, and so spoke to him about it, at which Foulkes 'vehemently denied it, and being willing to clear himselfe of that aspercion sent for his wife unto him, and when she came, asked her if he had struck or beaten her, and she utterly denied and then protested that it was false. Then [Foulkes] charging her with speaking thereof unto some of her neighbours, she confessed that she had declared that he had given her a bobb upon her lipp, and that it was true, and showed [Wall] her lipp, but [he] could not discerne the least hurt or scarr upon her lipp, and afterwards they were kind and friendly each to other.'[113] In considering this incident we must bear in mind that domestic discipline was normal practice at the time, and that if Isabella, a respectable country vicar's wife, was indeed drunk on a Saturday dinner time in Shrewsbury this would have attracted comment in itself were it not for the greater notoriety of Foulkes' own situation.

Another yeoman, Andrew Walker, had noticed Ann amongst a group of Stanton Lacy inhabitants, including Somerset Wall, at the Three Tuns Tavern. He and Foulkes had entered the room where Ann was and stayed there for about half an hour, but Ann and Foulkes had no conversation in private. Walker and Foulkes then left, leaving Ann among company at the Three Tuns, which was but a short walk across the square from the Fox Inn.[114]

On the following day, Sunday, Isabella rode home to Stanton Lacy with Walker, 'and was chearfull and merry upon the way homewards'; and Edward Smalman was able to add that on the night after Isabella had left, both he and Foulkes had not only spent the night at the Fox Inn, but were together in the same room. The next day they rode home, overtaking Ann at Church Stretton, where all had dismounted for refreshment 'at the house of one Berry'; and after their rest Smalman, another lawyer, Foulkes, and Ann, had all travelled home together as a party.[115]

The scant details of this excursion leave much to conjecture, but interested gossips could easily construe a suspected assignation between Foulkes and Ann, merely in the knowledge that Isabella had ridden home on the Sunday leaving both her husband and Ann in the county town. However, with so many neighbours and acquaintances present this would have been very difficult to engineer in an era where privacy was almost non-existent. Foulkes presumably had further business with lawyers in Shrewsbury on the Monday, but the episode does give us a colourful glimpse of a weekend excursion to Shrewsbury, of local interest in the court hearings, and of the impact of the chatter of uncharitable tongues.

A RESPITE

'I procured to my self some false quiet, and so deceived my self as well as others'

What action was taken against William Hopton following this is not recorded, other than in the Grand Jury finding for the plaintiffs; so what the immediate consequences were for him is yet unknown, although he evidently remained free. All that is certain is that, by the end of October 1677, Hopton 'for his misscariages was forced to Leave his Country', meaning that he had absconded from Stanton Lacy, supposedly taking with him about £1000 of Lord Craven's money.[116] The Court Book merely has the Latin annotation 'fugit' in the margin – that is 'he has fled'.

The impact of all this upon the proceedings against Foulkes was dramatic. With the prime ringleader now discredited, and presumably being actively sought by the authorities, the case against Foulkes must have appeared greatly compromised. An itemised schedule of Foulkes' defence costs was drawn up at this point, although for how long a period is not stated, but it adds up to a total of £25 17s. 4d.[117] An agricultural labourer at that time would have earned no more than about £17 in a year.

As a result of this setback, Francis Hutchinson, the unfortunate 'promoter' of the action, now lost his nerve, unsure as he had been from the start about the whole enterprise, and became desperate to disentangle himself. On the 12th November 1677 he signed his lengthy statement, in part already quoted above, complaining of being 'inveigled' into acting as promoter in order that his cousins the Hoptons would be able to give evidence.[118] 'They sollicited mee, and I out of ignorance complyed with them, and the rather because I was perswaded by Mr Cornwall theyre proctor soe to doe'.

It seems likely that Hutchinson had already been contemplating his withdrawal some time before, and at the end of October he had communicated his misgivings to Cornwall, who now tried to pressure him into staying with the case, warning him that 'if I did not proceede, Mr Foulkes would have charges against me, but if I went on, it should Cost me nothing'. Hutchinson nevertheless appears to have taken independent advice, and swore his affidavit before Thomas Crumpe of Ludlow, 'one of the masters in the High Court of Chancery'.

In his declaration Hutchinson also revealed that he had witnessed money changing hands prior to the hearing before the bishop at Croft Castle, when one of the bishop's servants was apparently bribed in order to introduce them to the bishop, saying that he would 'as much as could be stand theyre secret freinde to his Lordship'. He added that Richard Chearme had latterly tried to persuade him to continue as promoter, but asked that if he did withdraw then he was to mention Chearme's name as little as possible! Hutchinson nonetheless believed him to be 'the most violent and bitter of them all'.

Chearme's motives in these proceedings are less easy to understand, although Foulkes' earlier assault and battery on him probably explains a great deal. He does, though, seem very much to have been the Hoptons' creature, and Foulkes noted that from the outset he was 'engaged to doe nothinge without the Consent and advise' of the Hoptons, and that everything he did was through their 'informacion and instigacion'. Chearme, who could not sign his own name,

A brass halfpenny token (left), issued by Edward Miles, senior, of Ludlow in 1665. This is typical of the small change struck to the order of at least sixteen Ludlow merchants and tradesmen, and produced to make up for the deficit in small coinage due to neglect by the Crown. Tokens like these would have been very familiar to Foulkes during the early years of his incumbency, their use only finally abolished by Act of Parliament in 1672.

Isabella Foulkes' elder brother, the mercer William Colbatch of Worcester, also issued several, including a halfpenny (right) in 1667.

may well have been illiterate, and so in awe of them; but he was also said to have 'Gloryed very much in the ruine' of Foulkes, saying that 'this business should be talked of after they were Deade and gone, for that they had Lived to route the Parson of Staunton Lacy... and further sayd he would for the future teach the Parsons of Staunton Lacy how to Carry and Demeane themselves...'!

His position as Elizabeth's tenant at Hammonds Farm had fast become impossible, and he left after three years in about May of 1677.[119] Meanwhile, Foulkes now triumphantly quoted Hutchinson's affidavit in full in his defence submissions, heard before the court in February 1678.

In the wake of the apparent collapse of their case, it seems that Hutchinson was not alone among the combinators to be feeling exposed and vulnerable, and in March 1678 it was Martha Dovey's turn to be presented before the court. This was for misbehaviour in church, she having caused 'several disturbances by entring forcibly into other mens seats, and there behaving herself very rudely and irreverently by pulling, halling, and laughing, and other indecent and irreligious behaviour, much to the interruption of the minister and the congregacion'.[120] In the light of recent events, this does sound rather suspiciously as if 'Goody' Dovey might have been seeking comfort in a little too much liquid refreshment.

Despite Hutchinson's withdrawal, the case did not entirely collapse, for Cornwall himself now took over the role of promoter. This may have been in part to protect Hutchinson, but it is quite clear that it was the Church authorities that were far from happy to let things rest. Cornwall evidently was a not a man who was going to be beaten; he knew all the facts of the case, and he must have felt that with careful management there were still further opportunities for some success. His first action was to concentrate on proving the existence of Ann's illegitimate child, and so a new set of depositions were laid before the court in July 1678, presenting Ann for being delivered of a baby girl at West Felton, and for sending the child away to nurse at Llansantffraid, where she still contributed to the infant's maintenance. The question of the identity of the father was for once temporarily set aside.

With their enemies apparently now in confusion, in around February 1678 Foulkes and Ann had obviously felt relaxed enough to have yet another assignation in private, and recklessly their 'celebration' had taken a very physical form. The consequences of this union, nine short months later, were to be disastrous. The lovers' undoing, however, was also in part brought about by a curious mixture of chance and coincidence, for on Wednesday the 14th August 1678, a certain John Brabant was buried in Ludlow parish churchyard. He was but a poor man, and we know practically nothing about him.[121] Nonetheless, in another twist in this story, the passing of this humble pauper in Ludlow was also to be part of the chain of events that was, eventually, to end in the humiliation and death of Robert Foulkes.

CHAPTER 9

Somerset Brabant

'... pulling off his shoes that he might not be heard or discovered, went into another chamber adjoyning, and looking through a lardg hole in the wall divideing both chambers, and with his hand turning aside the hangings, did see Robert and Ann togeather upon the bedd ...'

Somerset Brabant (1641–1682), or *Sumarsat* Brabant as he signed himself, was a man of modest origins, and yet had a crucial part to play in this story. Although a joiner by trade, he was clearly literate, and by 1678 had worked for some years as a chamberlain, or room attendant, for Bridget Walker, innkeeper at the old Talbot Inn in Sydbury, Worcester. The

Talbot, now a city hotel and pub standing almost opposite the cathedral, was then one of the largest inns in Worcester during the 17th-century.[122] Today, concealed behind an unexceptional modern exterior, there survives the heart of the timber-framed building with which Brabant would have been very familiar, the flimsy interior wattle and plaster panelled walls offering but little privacy. Little did Foulkes and Ann know it but Brabant, to mix metaphors, was a time bomb fizzing away in the woodwork on a very slow fuse, and the chamberlain would dramatically and disastrously change their lives. The fact that he had suppressed what he knew for some four years suggests that he probably never intended to reveal it.

Although his depositions appear scandalized and disapproving, the moralising tone of his words seems more likely to have been put into his mouth by the lawyers who stood over him, one of whom was none other than the chancellor of the Diocese, Sir Timothy Baldwyn. Brabant was clearly placed in a somewhat precarious position, since he himself ran the risk of being accused of not informing the authorities, and of merely being a common peeping Tom – which it seems is probably exactly what he was. Willing or unwilling, he was obliged to tell the authorities all he knew only six days after the burial of his father, although the circumstances leading to Brabant's revelations can now only be surmised.

He was the third son of John Brabant and Anne Cooke, who were married at Culmington in October 1635, but had settled in Ludlow by the end of 1636.[123] Their five known

Opposite: This woodblock illustration, from a contemporary ballad sheet in the Pepys Library, shows a young couple keeping an illicit tryst at an inn. Many taverns of the period doubled as brothels, and assignations were commonplace in the relative anonymity of the larger towns. (*Reproduced by permission of the Master and Fellows of Magdelene College, Cambridge*).

children were all born in the town by 1645, but the suspension of the parish registers during the Commonwealth may conceal whether there were ever any more. Somerset was baptized in the parish church on the 4th April 1641, and in his childhood most likely witnessed all the terrors of the siege and bombardment of Ludlow, culminating in its surrender to Parliament in June of 1646.[124] From his evidence it is apparent that he knew both Foulkes and Ann well, at least by sight, and so therefore was almost certainly aware of Foulkes' marriage to Isabella in 1657. By the age of 26 Brabant had left Ludlow, and in 1667 was living in the parish of St. Michael in Bedwardine, Worcester, for in that year he put himself apprentice to William Barnard, a joiner and trunkmaker in the parish of St. Helens.[125]

Six months afterwards he was married by licence, at Spetchley near Worcester, to Barnard's daughter Anne, and the couple later had at least five children.[126] In 1678 he was still living in St. Helens, and we find him and his family in modest accommodation in Bull Alley, off High Street.[127]

Then in August of that year his father had died, and Somerset Brabant made what was perhaps an infrequent visit to be with his mother in his home town. On the 14th John Brabant was buried, after which it seems likely that Somerset would have been catching up with news and gossip, probably in one of the local taverns.

Talk would have got around to the subject of the long-standing scandal of Foulkes and Ann Atkinson; and Brabant, who knew them both, may have rashly revealed that he'd known all about this for years, because Foulkes and Ann had spent a night together at the Talbot in Worcester four years before, and that he had seen it all. Walls may well have had ears, and within a matter of hours Cornwall must have known that his long sought-after first-hand witness had just surfaced.

Brabant was taken before the chancellor in person, closely questioned, and made to sign two statements. The first, for the case against Ann, completed on the 20th of August, is scrappier and in the form of a draft, with numerous alterations and insertions showing careful reworking, but witnessed by Sir Timothy Baldwyn himself. The second, signed on the following day, is almost identical, although it dwells slightly more on Foulkes' involvement, and is a relatively fair copy.[128] There is no doubt that Brabant's testimony was the crucial evidence that Cornwall was so long awaiting, and its effects were immediate because on that first day, the 20th, Baldwyn had promptly issued an order banning Foulkes from preaching in Ludlow parish church.[129]

Brabant's story makes fascinating reading, in places explicit yet touching, and puts further flesh on the bones of our knowledge of the hapless lovers' affair. The time described is that during Ann's absence from Stanton Lacy over two years, following the delivery of the child at West Felton, when she and Foulkes were supposed to have been miles apart from one another.

At about Michaelmas (at the end of September) in 1674, Foulkes and Ann had arrived at the Talbot on the same day, Ann accompanied by one of Lady Craven's maidservants. Foulkes, calling for a room, was directed to one that was immediately next to that in which Ann and the maid were staying. Foulkes then enquired after Ann, and she joined him in his chamber, at which time he ordered a supper, asking that it should be brought up to them. They remained alone together; and Brabant, going in and out of the room several times to prepare it, 'and very well knowing them both', noticed 'much intimacy and familiarity betwixt them as kissing hugging and embraceing'. He also noticed that the bed had been 'very much tumbled', and therefore suspected that 'they had some further intention'.

From hereon the scene is reminiscent of a Restoration comedy. Pulling off his shoes so that he might neither be heard nor discovered, the chamberlain then tiptoed into another adjoining room where there was a large hole in the wall, and putting his hand through the hole was able to pull aside the hangings that lined the walls of Foulkes' room so that he could see all that took place.

Foulkes and Ann were by now upon the bed, 'stirring and labouring as in the very Act of uncleanness, after which manner they continued near the space of a Quarter of an hower'. After a brief rest, intimacy resumed for about the same time as before, and then they separated and, sitting close to one another, 'both fell into a passion of weeping, & continued a Quarter of an hower not speaking to one another', or so as Brabant could hear. 'And then the table being laid and supper brought up they did eat and drink together and were very pleasant and merry all supper time' while Brabant attended upon them, and 'still observed their more than ordinary familiarity'.

With supper cleared away, the chamberlain now returned to his former vantage point to see that Foulkes had blown out the candle, and was now sitting in a chair with his arms tightly about Ann who was between his legs, with her dress pulled up. There they stayed in the firelight for about two hours, 'kissing and clipping with much vigour and earnestness', during which time Ann would smile at him and often say: 'Fie, fie, for God sake be quiet!', and more enigmatically: 'Doe you think this is handsome?'. Several times Ann said in a loud voice 'Good Night, Good Night', as if to make the maid believe that she was trying to leave, and return next door to her room.

At length near midnight Ann earnestly begged Foulkes that he would never reveal what had passed between them, 'which he promised to do, but she told him that she would not believe unless he would swear so much to her, whereupon they ... kneeling down together upon the hearth before the fire, solemnly vowed and mutually protested to each other', after which they parted, and Ann returned to her room.

On the following morning, Brabant encountered the maid who told him that Foulkes had entered the room where Ann was in bed, and had 'thrust his hand into the bed and felt Ann's naked thighs and other parts of her body, and that he endeavoured to touch or feel the said maid which made her leap out of the bed and leave them together whilst she dressed herself in the same chamber'. Foulkes paid the bills for both rooms, and after meeting with Ann for a short time, they all took horse and departed. Brabant however subsequently heard and believed that Foulkes and Ann had also been 'intimate and familiar together at the Crown Inn, and other places in the said city of Worcester'.

THE NET CLOSES

By the 6th September 1678, proceedings were now once again in preparation against Foulkes himself, and two simple straightforward local witness statements, from Charles Pearce and Richard Hopton senior, were collected by Cornwall. These carefully avoided being bogged down by anything contentious by merely referring to 'common report' within Stanton Lacy, and the local understanding of the illegitimate child born at West Felton at the parsonage house, baptized by Francis Atkinson, Ann's brother, and sent away to nurse over the Welsh border.

Meanwhile further enquiries, pursued as a result of a commission of the Bishop of Coventry and Lichfield at West Felton, met with much less success, and all the witnesses questioned, including the women who were involved in delivering the baby, having once already been exhaustively interrogated three months before by a Justice of the Peace, now stubbornly refused to make any further comment before the Church authorities. The most co-operative was the young farmer, Edward Walker, resident in West Felton for six years but born in Stanton Lacy, and brother to Andrew Walker, who would only say that he had heard the story of the birth but not

One of the earliest surviving photographs of the nave of St. Laurence's parish church, Ludlow, probably taken in the summer of 1858, before its 'restoration'. Foulkes was banned from preaching here in August 1678. The gloomy interior conveys something of the atmosphere of the nave as a preaching auditorium, as it was in Foulkes' day, although the organ and galleries are of about a century after his time. Photograph probably taken by Thomas Jones of Ludlow.

of when it had happened. He, his wife, and several others had certainly been questioned before Robert Owen, Justice of the Peace, but what had been said he could not now remember, although when he was questioned he remembered saying that he knew nothing except what others had told him![130]

The final surviving document in the sequence, dated the 1st October 1678, is a draft list of twelve articles in the case against Ann, summarising the story of the illegitimate baby, the continuing affair, and Foulkes' and Ann's cruelty to Isabella, but also incorporating new evidence lately acquired. It has been carefully assembled, brick by brick, to build a damning case that brings in the fresh allegations, and leaves very little room for manoeuvre.

It is now also clear that the prosecution have come into possession of love correspondence, and Ann is accused of writing 'severall amorous and enticeinge Letteres' to Foulkes, in one or more of which she invited him to come to her, appointing a place or places where Foulkes and she might meet privately together unsuspected. '[You] did further declare by your lettere that you did hope... Foulkes and you in a shorte tyme might be more free, and Love one another without controle...'. This greatly begs the question as to who, within Foulkes' household, might have had the opportunity to come upon this very private correspondence, and then hand it over to Cornwall. The finger very much points at Isabella.

Moreover, the new draft directly accuses Foulkes of having got at the witnesses questioned before the bishop's commission at West Felton, and maintains that he had applied 'himselfe to all or att least some of the witnesses in the said Comission ... and did endeavour to perswade (as much as in him lay) the witnesses to depose noe otherwaies then how hee directed them, ... and what answears they should give to the questions which should be demanded of them'. It also claims that at least one of Ann's brothers 'was presente in the place or roome when... Mr Foulkes gave such direccions or Instruccions'. The implications of all this for Foulkes' career in the Church were now grave. It is difficult to see how he could have successfully defended himself, and his precarious position must have been becoming all too readily apparent.

By this time, however, Foulkes and Ann had an even more urgent matter on their minds, with the danger of the discovery of the impending arrival of yet another child becoming ever more likely.

Hitherto, in addition to their first infant, there had been other pregnancies, but these apparently had been successfully aborted.[131] Despite their best efforts, this one was strong and resisted miscarriage. What happened next we mostly have as fragments from the contemporary printed sources.[132]

Opposite: A mid-18th century engraving showing a gentleman prisoner being shown into his room at Newgate, while its previous occupant has been released and can be seen departing through the door. This shows the interior of the building that Foulkes got to know well, rebuilt in 1666 after the Great Fire, and his accommodation would have been very similar. While a fire burns cheerfully enough in the grate, the macabre model gallows over the fireplace would have been a chilling reminder of the occupant's possible ultimate destination. (*Reproduced by permission of the Department of Prints and Drawings, British Museum*)

CHAPTER 10

To London, and Nemesis

'The Jurors for the Lord King upon their oaths present that a certain Ann Atkinson, impiously within the parish of St. Martin-in-the-Fields, in the County of Middlesex, a spinster, was pregnant with a certain girl infant on the 11th day of December, in the thirtieth year of the reign of our Lord Charles the Second, by the Grace of God King of England, Scotland, France and Ireland, Defender of the Faith...'

Exactly when Ann was moved away to London was not recorded. An 18th-century source, not entirely trustworthy but possibly based on then-surviving Old Bailey Sessions Papers, related that all the means that Foulkes could think of 'to procure abortion were now tried, and they all proved ineffectual; so that they must be both exposed to scandal, unless she could be removed to some convenient place, remote from the eyes of the world, and from the jealousies of Mrs Foulkes, where she might be delivered of her burden, which was not yet perceived. A plausible excuse for his going up to London was soon formed ...'.[133] The writer of *The Execution of Mr. Rob. Foulks* may imply in his opening lines that she and Foulkes were together in London by November, although wrongly asserting that this was when the child was born. *A true and perfect Relation* merely comments that Foulkes, not willing that the neighbours should be acquainted with the impending birth, 'brought her (under pretence of preferring her) to London, and took lodging for her in York Buildings in the Strand, resolving to stay with her till the pains of the delivery should be over'.

However this, as with all the printed sources, makes no mention whatever of Ann's name, nor gives any clues to her identity, but misleadingly states that Foulkes was her 'guardian', and merely describes her as a 'young Gentlewoman, committed to his charge'.

This account was in fact published after the court case and her acquittal and, as we shall see, appears to have been derived from misinformation laid before the court by Ann's defence during the trial.[134] She was, after all, by this time twenty-eight years old. Bearing in mind the saga of their involvement so far, it is difficult to believe that her family knew nothing of what was going on, nor of why she was being whisked off to London. While it is not impossible that her well-being was committed to Foulkes' care by her step-mother, whatever the case may be he certainly had a moral responsibility for Ann's safety and welfare.

What happened next was revealed before a full trial at the Old Bailey in front of 'the two Lords Chief Justices assisted with four of the Judges, the Lord Mayor and Recorder of

London'.[135] No detailed account of the trial seems to have survived, and apparently no copy of the relevant Sessions Papers is still in existence; so our only insight into what they stood accused of is gleaned from the indictment recorded in the pre-trial Gaol Delivery Roll for the Middlesex Sessions, a carefully compiled matter-of-fact account in Latin, which makes for sombre reading.[136] Until recently it has perhaps gone unnoticed because it is indexed not under Foulkes but under his co-defendant Ann.

In summary, the jury found that she, a spinster, had been present in the parish of St. Martin-in-the-Fields, and pregnant with a 'bastard' girl child that, by divine providence, was born there alive on the 11th December 1678.

Secondly, that Robert 'Fowlkes', clerk, and Ann, not holding God before their eyes, were moved and led astray at the instigation of the Devil, and that the baby was delivered by force.

Then Foulkes with deliberate malice had struck the child in the throat with a knife, causing a mortal wound three inches in length, and half in depth, and that the child had died immediately as a result. The jury therefore declared upon their oaths their belief that Foulkes and Ann had, out of malice and with premeditation, killed and murdered the child against the peace of the Lord King.

This monstrous act all too clearly reveals the utter desperation in Foulkes' state of mind.

He had then departed for home on his own soon after the murder, but was pursued to Shropshire and brought back to London, where both were held in the typhus-infested hellhole known as Newgate prison. Gentlefolk of means could at least spare themselves the worst of the utter squalor and degradation of Newgate by paying the keeper to occupy the better accommodation, and obtain some comforts or 'garnish' as it was called. Both Foulkes and Ann, however, would have paid dearly for this, and it was notorious for being some of the most exorbitant lodging in London.

When they came before the Sessions, both pleaded Not Guilty; but during the course of the trial Ann strenuously distanced herself from Foulkes, whose situation may well have appeared doomed from the outset and, not surprisingly, she fought a personal battle to save her own neck.

As a consequence, two different versions of what had happened are left to us. To give the narrative according to *A true and perfect Relation*:

> ...at length the fatal hour of her dreaded travel [travail] approacht, and she by her lowd shrieks began to call for the welcome assistance of her own sex, ... but that it seems was utterly denied her by Mr. Foulks, who sternly oblig'd her to silence, protesting no body should perform that Office but himself. What pangs the poor woman endured by so painful a Delivery is best judg'd by those who have been experienced in those labours; but the wicked intent of this barbarous usage, could referr to nothing but the designed destruction of the unfortunate babe, whom he no sooner received into the world, but cruelly cram'd it down a house of office.

Foulkes on the other hand, in his printed confession, directly implicated Ann in the infant's destruction, declaring 'Upon the word of a dying Man, That both her Eyes did see, and her Hands did Act in all that was done'.[137]

He also told a visitor, Dr. William Lloyd, that after delivering the baby he had asked Ann what he should do with it, to which she had replied that he should kill it, and 'gave him the knife with which he killed it, and when he had thrown it into the house of office, she went half an hour after with a curtain rod with which she thrust it down out of sight.'[138]

Admittedly we only have Foulkes' word for this, but if this is true then Ann most effectively feigned innocence before the court during the trial, remaining emphatic 'that upon her delivery he took the Child away, as she thought to provide a Nurse, and she in no condition to follow him, knew not what was done to it'.[139] Another account affirmed that Ann had claimed she was 'altogether ignorant of what he had done, till he himself had informed her what he had done with the murdered infant'.[140]

For their part, apparently on Lord Chief Justice Scrogg's direction, the jury chose to believe that when Foulkes had left Ann, the child was still alive, and so she testifying that she was 'not in the least consenting to the Murder, was both pittied and acquitted' by the court.

It is not only in the Gaol Delivery Roll but also in a letter, written some years afterwards, that we find reference to the knife wound.[141] Smothering the baby, though still barbarous, might at least have left open the possibility that she had been stillborn; but Foulkes appears to have trusted sufficiently in Ann's complicity not to reveal the hiding place of the child's remains. The group of streets off the Strand known as York Buildings, Nicholas Barbon's then recently-built development on the site of York Place, was very close to the Thames, and in putting the body down the house of office – a privy – Foulkes and Ann may have assumed that the little corpse would be on its way to being washed down into the river.

This was apparently a common fate of unwanted babies, and so almost certainly the first place where searchers would look. It is also evident, from the accounts, that Foulkes had departed for Shropshire 'the next morning when as he thought he had done his business very securely... but had not long been there, before the indisposition of the green woman gave her attendant sufficient evidence she had been Delivered

The elegant frontages in Buckingham Street, one of the group of five streets that were together known as 'York Buildings'. Samuel Pepys lived first at number 12 from 1679, and then later at number 14 from 1687. The fronts were updated during the Georgian period.

of a Child, which at last she confest'.[142] That Foulkes had left Ann in London after the murder, virtually on her own to cope with the situation, can only have compounded the court's attitude to him. Chance, too, apparently played its part in the discovery of the crime, which we are told rather cryptically was revealed only 'by a Strange Providence'.[143]

We do not know whether the Atkinson family rallied around Ann at the trial or engaged her defence lawyers; but, whatever their attitude to her, it would not have been in their interests simply to have abandoned her. If she had been condemned for this murder, it would have had a direct effect on them by association. She was certainly represented by her own counsel independently, and the effect of Ann's evidence was to deliver Foulkes' head to the court on a platter; indeed it was said that he was convicted 'by no other but her single Testimony'.

Following his sentence, however, Foulkes neither hesitated to admit his guilt, nor shrank from freely acknowledging revulsion at his act, for he wrote: 'To destroy an innocent Babe had cruelty enough in it; but to offer violence to the fruit of ones own body, was such a monstrous piece of barbarity, as admits not of a parallel'. Ann in contrast, after the trial, 'was as Jolly as he was sad', and 'enterteining her Lawyers at the Tavern'.[144]

Seventeenth-century justice was a decidedly blunt instrument, the trial process being designed to secure conviction rather than search for truth; and so while Foulkes acknowledged that justice had been done, he still felt ill-served by a process in which he was publicly accused and condemned for some things of which, he maintained, he was innocent.

Despite London then being in the grip of the hysteria of the Popish Plot, with Titus Oates still in his ascendancy, it is clear that this trial was the talk of the city, and the public galleries were filled with onlookers. Foulkes wrote of this in his pamphlet *An Alarme for Sinners*, referring to a visit by:

> ...one Mr. Smith the Ordinary of Newgate. He was pleased to tell me (but in Private) that he observed me at my Tryal Gazing about the Court and the Galleries, where sate several Gentlewomen. I confess I was formerly too apt to delight in such sights ... but at that time I had other thoughts and Apprehensions: the cause of that diversion was to spy out some Witnesses I thought Material, which though they were in Court I could not find, and so lost their Evidence. This (t'is very probable) may have been the observation of others as well as Mr. Smith, therefore I insert this just Apology.[145]

Various other rumours and stories circulated during the hearing, some apparently promoted by Ann or her defence. Foulkes wrote that his 'Partner in the Guilt and Tryal, though not in the Condemnation, was pleased to load me with several Calumnies. I will only note those that the Court insisted on, and I hear are yet discoursed to my prejudice in the City'. The first, which he took particular exception to, was that Ann's father had committed her to him as her guardian in her 'Minority and Childhood.'

He continued:

> This report is so generally spread, and indeed sounds so ill, that several since my Tryal have discoursed it as a great Aggravation; to commit so foul a thing against so Great a Trust, and some have repaired to me for Satisfaction; to whom I then gave as I do now the World this Account, That Her Father was a Gentleman whom I never saw, or had the least Intercourse with. There are two more Accusations, which I would not so much as name, but that I found them the only Ingredients that Imbittered my Cup both at my Trial, and at my Sentence; The one was, That I should attempt and endeavour to vitiate her at Nine years old.

An Alarme

FOR

SINNERS:

Containing

The Confeſſion, Prayers, Letters, and laſt Words of

Robert Foulkes,

Late Miniſter of *Stanton-Lacy* in the County of *Salop*; who was Tryed, Convicted, and Sentenced, at the Seſſions in the *Old Bayly*, *London*, *January* 16th 167$\frac{8}{9}$, and Executed the 31ſt following.

With an Account of his LIFE.

Publiſhed from the Original, Written with his own hand, during his Reprieve, and ſent by him at his Death to Doctor *Lloyd*, Dean of *Bangor*.

Let him that thinketh he ſtandeth, take heed leſt he fall. 1 Cor. 10.12.

Licenſed, *Jan.* 29. 1678.

LONDON,

Printed for *Langley Curtis*, on *Ludgate-Hill*, 1679.

The title page of Foulkes' *An Alarme for Sinners*, shown here in its original state, when licensed for publication on the 29th of January 1678/79. After the Act expired, later copies omitted all reference to this licence, and there were further variations in the wording, showing that printing was extended over a number of months.

The other, That I had for that purpose corrupted her Judgement, and misinformed her Conscience to believe Polygamy lawful... I confess I have sins that exceed them, yet I never was guilty of either of these, and in the midst of an abundance of Guilt, I find a little Comfort in this...[146]

This manipulated version of events was still in print during the 18th-century when Captain Charles Johnson published his *A General History of the Lives and Adventures of the Most Famous Highwaymen, Murderers etc.* in 1734, reprinted in 1926.[147] This brief account of Foulkes story, possibly based on the lost Sessions Papers, described Ann as being a 'young gentlewoman of a considerable fortune, who had been left an infant by her parents, [and] was committed to [Foulkes'] care by her executors, as to a man who, they trusted, would not only deal justly by her, but also instruct her betimes in the principles of religion...'

Had Foulkes really been Ann's guardian then surely much would have been made of it during the consistory court proceedings, not just by the prosecution but also by the defence. The fact that her stepmother was still very much alive is completely ignored; and no mention is ever made of Ann's first child four years before, although this last is scarcely surprising since both had in public vehemently denied its existence for the past three years. The text then goes on to claim that she was less than twenty years old at her trial, when she was plainly nearer twenty-nine.

Short of finding a copy of the original Sessions Papers we will never know for certain what his judges believed, but these may be some of the misrepresentations that Foulkes claimed the court had 'insisted' upon.

Immediately after the trial, there were evidently others who were as concerned that he should not stand condemned for things he had never done, for the title page of *A true and perfect Relation* stated that it was at least in part published 'for to satisfy all people that are incensed with base and foolish Reports on this unhappy man'.

Those who stood most to lose by association were his fellow clergy, and, for the Church, Foulkes' very public condemnation and impending execution were certainly seen as serious cause for loss of confidence. This was also at a time when the clergy were under increasing attack for their aloofness, and their disdain for the popular religious attitudes of their parishioners. For that reason, once the course of justice was clear, some senior churchmen immediately took matters in hand to set in motion a damage-limitation exercise.

Foulkes wrote that upon the very evening after his sentence, the 16th of January 1678/79, he received the first of a number of visits from Dr. William Lloyd, at that time Dean of Bangor, but who was in the following year to be installed as Bishop of St. Asaph. At this time Lloyd also just happened to be vicar at the church of St Martin-in-the-Fields, the parish within which the murder had taken place.

Another visitor, according to Anthony à Wood, was Dr. Gilbert Burnet, Lloyd's close friend, and subsequently Bishop of Salisbury during the reign of William and Mary.[148] Foulkes was to have died on Wednesday the 22nd of January, with other condemned prisoners, but after Dr. Lloyd had approached the Bishop of London to petition the King, a reprieve of nine days was granted.

In the meantime Foulkes had already set about fulfilling Lloyd's advice that he should 'wipe off all I could of the Scandal and Reproach which my Vicious Life and Ignominious Death reflected upon my Function; and both these, he told me, could not be more Effectually performed, than by a full Confession of my manifold Enormities. I then resolved upon it; and as soon as I could procure Pen and Paper, set about it'.

The resulting outpouring of self-castigation and remorse, entitled *An Alarme for Sinners*, was widely read in its day and subsequently, the papers having been given by Foulkes to William Lloyd shortly before his execution.[149] Indeed this heartfelt declaration of his penitence does seem to have reassured fellow clergy, for the Puritan minister and early political journalist Roger Morrice, while only briefly noting his condemnation and execution, was clearly gratified that Foulkes 'gave very hopefull evidence of his true Repentance for such great and scandalous offences.'[150] It is evidently Foulkes who gave it its title, used as the heading on the first page of the text, and what is certain is that he specifically wrote it for publication.

Another small tract, *The Execution of Mr. Rob. Foulks*, explained that he had 'imployed the few moments he had to live, in Writing down his Meditations, and giving a warning to Sinners, by his sad, but remarkable Example; and directing several Letters to his Wife, Children, Parishoners and other friends, which being Compleated under his own hand, and delivered to very Worthy and Reverend Persons, are to be made publick'. To this was added the text of his last confession and speech from the gallows, a copy of which 'having it ready Written, (with his own hand) he there delivered to a Minister present, to be faithfully Printed with the rest of his Papers which are now in the Press, and within very few days will be made publick'.

According to the earlier versions of the title page, it was licensed for publication on the 29th January 1678/79, two days before Foulkes' death, and appears to have been printed in large numbers and over an extended period.[151] We are also told that Foulkes 'prepared an excellent Prayer fitted for his occasion, which he transcribed with his own hand, and caused to be sent to most Churches in London, on the 30th of

January, that being the Fast day strictly kept for the Murder of King Charles the First, so that by this means he was earnestly prayed for through the whole City'.[152]

With the exception of that of Anthony à Wood, the accounts of Foulkes' final moments on Friday the 31st of January are in general agreement. *A true and perfect Relation* tells that 'When the fatal and appointed day of Execution came, he was brought out of the Press-Yard about ten of the Clock in the morning, and in a Coach conveyed to Tyburn, accompanied thither with several Eminent Divines, who were mightily satisfied to see him cheerfully undergoe that great Work, with that constant Piety and Resolution which he had Exercised in Newgate. When he was got on the Ladder, he made a very excellent Speech to the People to disswade them from those wicked courses which had brought him to that ignominious End'. This is followed by a remarkably free version of Foulkes' last address which, when compared with his prepared text, would seem to have been largely improvised for want of better copy. An apology explains that 'His Speech was much longer, but the greatness of the crowd hindered us from hearing all, but the substance we have here Related.'.

John Dunton's *The Wonders of Free Grace* also remarks that 'he had the favour to be carried in a Coach to Tyburn, where a numerous croud attended as Spectators of his untimely fall; when being put into the Cart, he addressed himself to them...' The writer, either Dunton or an assistant, also claimed to have watched Foulkes die, 'his End being very penitent when he had a true sight of his Sins, as we find in his own writings, and by what we were an Eye-witness at the place of Execution'.[153] In this final journey by coach, usually allowed to the condemned of 'quality', Foulkes was at least spared the very public spectacle and humiliation of being hauled to Tyburn in a cart. The January weather may also have been a consideration, and the Ordinary's coach used as much to shelter those that went with him. Anthony à Wood's account of the event, however, creates a rather different impression of his end, and was presumably based on the stories doing the rounds in Oxford. In *Athenae Oxonienses* he said that Foulkes was 'executed at Tyburn, not with other common felons, but by himself, in the presence of a very few persons'; and elsewhere, in Wood's contemporary journal-notes, Foulkes 'did not die with the rabble, but very privatly at Tyburne'.[154]

This was practically impossible, and the main accounts seem to agree that in fact a large crowd attended, although it appears to be true that he did not die in the company of other criminals, and thus it was not as big a public event as it might have been. It was also Wood who had remarked that 'Robert Fulk, sometime of Christ Church Oxford, got a maid with child. The child being still borne (as t'is said), he throw'd it in the privy house'.

Here Wood was probably merely reporting local gossip; and the idea that the baby was stillborn, and that the mother was, perhaps, merely a servant, was surely but wishful thinking amongst his clerical peers at Oxford. To be fair, however, none of the contemporary printed accounts either identified Foulkes' paramour or told in any detail how the baby had died.

Whatever his conduct and crime in life, Foulkes did die manifestly with courage and dignity. His humour did not desert him even in his farewell performance, and he managed to crack a black joke – a play on words: 'You may in me see' he said, 'what it is for one who was a Member of Christ, to make himself the Member of a Harlot'![155] After his short address to the crowd, we are told he 'pray'd very earnestly, and then freely submitted to the Execution of the Sentence'. Foulkes' death was a slow and painful one, for the scaffold had no drop. The accounts, both apparently written by eyewitnesses, talk variously of him being either 'got on the ladder' or 'put into the cart'.

Whether he was turned off the ladder by the hangman, or the cart merely driven away, dying was a slow process by strangulation and could take up to twenty minutes; and only after about an hour would the victim be cut down. Relatives, or possibly his fellow churchmen, then claimed the body, in exchange for a fee paid to the hangman, and Foulkes was 'brought back in a Coach, and that Evening decently (but privately) Interr'd at St. Giles'.

The burial register for the church of St. Giles-in-the-Fields, the parish within which Tyburn lay, simply records: '1678/9 31st January Robert Fouks Executed'.[156]

> Now the Lord be with you all, and have mercy upon my poor Soul; for which I desire you to pray with me and for me to the last moment of my life.

CHAPTER 11

Aftermath

'And now, my Dear Wife, I must bid thee, and all the World
farewell; and it grieves me more to part with thee and thine,
than all the world besides.'

At the news of the shocking events in London a stunned
silence had perhaps descended briefly upon Stanton Lacy, but
undoubtedly there will have been some rejoicing in certain
quarters, although many of the participators in Foulkes'
downfall had, for one reason or another, already left. Thereafter
the parish is likely to have been able to return to a comparatively
quiet normality that it had not enjoyed in nearly five years. His
successor as vicar, Thomas Greenhalgh M.A., was instituted
in the following July, but stayed for only four years; to be

replaced by Samuel Newborough M.A., who remained in the parish for some thirty-five years until his death in 1718.[157] In one of his final open letters, Foulkes had addressed himself to his successor, hoping that his patron would 'settle there a Man of worth and understanding, which may seem to make my well-meant Advice unnecessary'. He told him that:

> If You look over, once mine, now your, Study Door, you will find these words affixed:
>
> > Deus & Dies
> > Dic mihi cur Dei memor sis atque Diei?
> > Oro, Laboro."

In *The Wonders of Free Grace*, this was elegantly Englished in rhyme as:
> Tell me why these so joyn'd your mind possess
> Why God and time conjunctly you express:
> I pray and study, these require no less.

Referring to his parishioners, he wrote: 'You will find a great need of both prayers and diligence; they are such as require the Apostles sharp Reproof, and you may use it in the Pulpit, but take heed of it out, they will be led, but not driven. But to prepare your way, I have one request to propound to you, endeavour it, if not for mine, yet for your own sake. Labour to compose and draw up a wide Rent or Schism between the Parishioners; It may seem to commence, and bear no longer date but in my time, but I know 'tis much more Ancient, almost Hereditary to some of them.' Foulkes does not explain this, but while he had undoubtedly succeeded in splitting his parish, it may refer to far older divides that were reinforced, if not created, during the Civil War.

He also recommended that his successor speak directly and plainly to his flock: 'St. Paul's aim was to speak words easie to understand, *apta non alta*, which if you observe not, after many years you will find you have frustrated your own design...'. Perhaps this was the key to Foulkes' own success as a preacher. He ended: 'I have no more to add, but my Prayers, That you may be in that Place the Spiritual Father of a numerous Offspring, by begetting many Sons and Daughters unto God, and enjoy more Comfort and Tranquillity there than did Your Predecessour, R. Foulkes.'

Of Ann's fate little is at present known, not least of all whether she ever had to confront Foulkes' very public accusation that she was directly implicated in the murder, although it was something that Dr. William Lloyd clearly believed without question. We have heard that after her acquittal she was celebrating with her lawyers in London, and there she remained for at least three years. At that distance she also appears to have been immune from further action in the Ludlow court, and while she was away 'there was no farther proceeding against her'.

Ann then decided to return to Stanton Lacy during the summer of 1682, and 'having made friends in the Ecclesiastical Court, she made bold to appear, and there being nothing proved against her she was dismissed without any Censure'.[158] This was despite the fact that Isabella Foulkes had spoken to Sir Timothy Baldwyn, who had 'promised' her that 'he would make the wicked woman do penance in every Church in the diocese, or pay such a commutation as should maintain her and her four Children'. When Ann came before the court, however, Baldwyn 'was content not to be present'; and his deputy received an order to discharge her, although later that day he confessed to Isabella that he was ashamed of having done so.

Distressed and offended by this, Isabella approached William Lloyd, by now enthroned as Bishop of St. Asaph, and on the 3rd of January 1682/83 he wrote a scandalized letter to William Sancroft, the Archbishop of Canterbury.[159] In this, Lloyd gave an account of his interviews with Foulkes after the trial, showing that he clearly believed Foulkes' story of what had happened at York Buildings.

He had also seen Ann 'once or twice... in her lying in'; and his opinion of her was unequivocal, most of all deploring the fact that 'this horrible woman', 'that most flagitious woman', appeared to have escaped punishment of any sort, especially recently before the bishop's court. 'All good men are amaz'd at this,' he said, 'the Churches enemies triumph, and the Countrey hold their noses at our disciplin'. This doubtless refers to the resentment, not least on the influential part of the gentry and aristocracy, of the intrusive interference of the church in what they considered their private lives. There was also the tension between the parallel systems of the civil and church courts, where a person could be acquitted in one and yet harassed in another.

Lloyd's next letter to Sancroft, dated the 31st of January, acknowledges receiving a copy of Hereford's response to the archbishop, Lloyd expressing satisfaction to see that 'those who have little sense of Conscience or shame have yet some regard to your Grace's displeasure, and will do that for fear of it which they would not have done otherwise'. He continued: 'But now your Grace has been pleased to take notice of it, I doubt not somthing will be done for the removing of this horrible Scandall'.[160] Apparently on the basis of this, it has been asserted that Ann was excommunicated, but no evidence for this survives at Hereford; neither in Bishop Croft's registers, nor in the Caveat Books for the period.[161]

What happened to Ann after this is at present a mystery. Her move back to Stanton Lacy may have been necessary because in March 1681/82 Elizabeth appears to have become seriously ill, and 'being sick in body' she had made a new will. Ann was her first-named beneficiary, receiving a silver caudle cup and porringer, and all the furniture 'in a chamber called the yellow chamber' in Elizabeth's house.[162]

In the event of Elizabeth's death, in accordance with her father's will, Ann would also have received the great tithes of Stanton Lacy township, under the terms of Lord Craven's lease. Nor was Mary Hopton, the renegade niece, forgotten, for she was left five pounds 'to be payd her within six months of my decease'; so after William Hopton's departure, Mary may well have made her peace with her aunt.

In fact Elizabeth survived for a decade after Foulkes' execution, dying in June 1689 at the then ripe old age of 82, and willed that she be buried at Stanton Lacy 'as neare as may be to my deare husband Thomas'.

Ann's two elder brothers also appear to have weathered the storm. Parson Francis Atkinson became a pluralist, having been presented to his father's old rectory at Wistanstow in May of 1678, and adding that of Aston Botterell in October 1679. He died ten years later, in January 1689/90, and lies buried at Wistanstow.[163] John Atkinson the physician married Olive Davies, the widow of a Ludlow apothecary, in 1684, and acted as executor of the wills of both his brother and stepmother. He died suddenly while on a journey in September 1697, after being taken ill at the house of Thomas Monington at Sarnesfield in Herefordshire, surviving only long enough to make a simple nuncupative or verbal will in favour of his nephew.[164]His body was returned, and buried at Stanton Lacy.

What became of Foulkes' immediate family is at present a complete mystery. Not surprisingly, all reference in the Stanton Lacy parish registers to his wife and children ceases after 1679, although it appears that Isabella must have been in the Ludlow area because she heard from Baldwyn's deputy the same day that Ann had been discharged by the consistory court in 1682. At this time she may have been staying with her brother, John. Another possibility is that the family had moved to Worcester, where her other brother William had been living until his death in late 1676. In his will, Isabella was to inherit £10 if she outlived her husband within the lifetime of William's executors. Between 1678 and 1680 a 'Widdow Fookes' moved into premises in Bear Pott Lane in St Andrews parish, although she was possibly the Joan Foulkes who had previously lived nearby.[165]

Foulkes, in his last letter to his wife, commended her to 'thy good Brother; to whom, next God, I bequeath thee for Advice and Direction: Be governed by him'. Their 'four sweet Children' had been baptized at Stanton Lacy: Elizabeth, in November 1665; Samuel in December 1667; William in February 1670; and young Robert in January 1673.

It is puzzling that there is no mention of Samuel in his father's letter, only three of the children being mentioned by name – 'Betty', 'Billy', and 'Robin' – but in this they were urged 'to be dutiful to your Mother and Uncle'.[166] This uncle was almost certainly John Colbatch, Isabella's only known brother then surviving who, according to Martha Dovey, had been informed early on of Foulkes' involvement with Ann, and of their first child. Colbatch was a prominent member of Ludlow Corporation, and served three times as a town Bailiff. He was High Bailiff for the second time in 1702 when he died during his final term of office.

There is, however, no mention in his will of either Isabella or her family. A younger sister, Mary, had married but had left no known will.[167]

Despite her contribution to his downfall, Isabella appears to have remained attentive and constant to Foulkes to the end, and probably more so than he ever deserved.

He wrote to her:

I Rejoyce in the Entireness of thy Affection, which all the cold Water I threw upon it could not quench. The Constancy of it, especally in this Extremity, has given me the Comfort, and thee the Character of being one of the best of Wives.

She must have witnessed his arrest in Stanton Lacy, but whether his letter implies she had followed him to London, and was present during his imprisonment and trial, is far from clear. Isabella later contacted Dr. William Lloyd in 1682, so this perhaps suggests that she had met him at Newgate during Foulkes' confinement there. It was quite customary for relatives to attend an execution, if only to be on hand to claim the body and ensure decent burial. Whatever actually happened, his letter implies that they were at very least in contact.

There may therefore have been other private communication between them, but in this last public letter, perhaps as much written for the record, he asked her to 'remember only those days, when we were at a distance from that fatal Family'; and he was emphatic that she should keep the children away 'from that House at *Stanton*, there is nothing to be learnt there but Lying and Hypocrisie; and not only Opportunities, but Encouragements to Lust'. The house in mind is almost certainly Elizabeth's, but whether he was referring to Ann's presence as the 'encouragement', or was suggesting that Elizabeth had actually abetted him in his relationship with her, is open to question.

Evidence for the latter is decidedly thin in the court documents, although Cornwall did comment that it was to Elizabeth's 'scandall' that she had permitted them to meet so easily, presumably for not having enforced the bishop's admonition more effectively, and directly accused her of knowing much more than she was acknowledging. In public Elizabeth insisted upon her belief in Foulkes' and Ann's denials, although in private this would seem scarcely credible, but whether she actually *deliberately* turned a blind eye to what was going on, or just did not want to know, is left unresolved. Elizabeth certainly appears to have been over-indulgent with her stepdaughter in not having put her foot down and thrown Foulkes out long before. Ann on the other hand emerges as the manipulative spoilt youngest child, orphaned with two elder brothers, doted on by her late father, and so maybe pampered and indulged by her family after his death. Her stepmother therefore may well have had little control over Ann, if ever she had any; and it is not impossible that Isabella was the nearest thing to a real mother that Ann ever had.

There does seem little doubt, however, that Foulkes and Ann were besotted with one another. Today, in a more supportive and tolerant age, their affair will still have caused a local scandal, and Foulkes may well have been forced to resign his living, but at least the child would have lived – adopted, or raised by one or both parents.

For Foulkes, though, in the bitterness of his final shame, and despite the fact that he acknowledged that it was she who had been 'easily tempted' by him, Ann was the 'sad companion and partner' in his debaucheries, prepared for him by the Devil to be a 'constant temptation' to him. She was nothing but a 'harlot', a 'whorish woman', by whom he, a mere pathetic hapless man, was doomed to be ensnared and betrayed. It was Eve who listened to the serpent and ate the apple, and here yet again had caused Adam's downfall, and his ejection from the Garden of Eden. Adam, it seems, was too spineless to have had any say in the matter.

For a member of the clergy, the nature and brutality of Foulkes' crime may not be unique, nor the dire consequences in him being so publicly crushed by the full rigours of the law. John Atherton, Bishop of Waterford and Lismore, had been hanged in Dublin in December 1640 for sodomy; but after Foulkes' death, almost a century was to pass before another clergyman was to suffer at Tyburn, when no less than three were executed there within the space of two years. In June 1777 the celebrated preacher and author Dr William Dodd was hanged for forgery, having failed to get a reprieve; and five months later the Reverend Benjamin Russen, Master of the Charity School of St Matthew at Bethnal Green, died for the rape of a ten-year-old girl. Lastly, in April 1779, the Reverend James Hackman was hanged for shooting his lover, Miss Martha Reay, at Covent Garden. Although he was clearly deranged at the time, unfortunately she also just happened to be the mistress to the Earl of Sandwich!

There does, though, remain the question as to how unusual it was at this time for a parish priest such as Foulkes to become embroiled with the ecclesiastical courts, in particular when accused of immoral conduct or sexual adventures. The vast majority of presentations of clergy in the consistory courts concerned parochial affairs. These range from a lack of repairs to their church chancels or vicarages, to a poor standard of preaching, very occasionally neglect of their cure, unreasonable behaviour, and rather less infrequently drunkenness. Those accused of serious lapses in morality seem to have been a tiny minority, and it was perhaps the urban parishes, with all the distractions and temptations that towns offered, that potentially presented the greatest threat to a priest's morals.

One memorable example, exactly contemporary with Foulkes, is that of Richard Littleton, then curate to the rectory of St. Mary de Crypt in the city of Gloucester. He too was an able preacher, but appears to have had a predilection for fondling girls, in return for suitable offerings of money, at assignations in upstairs rooms at the more questionable local alehouses.[168] In June 1675, just at the time of Foulkes' activities in Stanton Lacy, Littleton was presented for having had an illegitimate child, in a dubious case that ended when the girl's mother retracted her complaint, probably aided by intimidation and gifts of money.

A number of witnesses were assembled on either side, with mostly influential character referees for Littleton, and the affair succeeded in splitting the local community. At around the same time, however, he had also implicated the local schoolmaster in another of his escapades, dragging him out of bed on the pretext of accompanying him to Barton Fair, but then suggesting a visit to the King's Arms, a well-known house of ill repute. Here his companion was obliged to watch while Littleton diverted himself with two of the landlord's sisters, but the schoolmaster subsequently lodged a complaint about Littleton before the consistory court.

It also emerged that Littleton had been previously presented in 1668 for drunkenness and lewd behaviour, and another seven years prior to that. There was also evidence that Littleton, like Foulkes, had organised his witnesses, some of them conniving with him into giving similar character testimonies before the court. Littleton was shortly afterwards ejected from St Mary de Crypt, not least to distance him from temptation. He was not, on the other hand, removed from holy orders, and once again the Church appeared to rally around one of its own if only to protect the reputation of the institution. He was evidently a pluralist, and managed to hold on to his vicarage at Longney, a mere six miles away.[169] Littleton was still there at the time of his death in 1715.

In the light of this, Somerset Brabant's graphic evidence, together with Foulkes having instructed witnesses, would very likely have resulted in him being promptly ejected from Stanton Lacy. Too much had happened in the parish during the previous four years to allow his bishop to let him remain in place. Even had the murder never happened, or Foulkes succeeded in covering up the arrival of the second child, the outlook for him would doubtless have been bleak. Had he stayed put he would have continued to divide the community, and it would have been almost impossible for him to command the respect necessary to remain an effective preacher in the general neighbourhood, let alone pastor of his own flock.

Foulkes knew that his career was in dire jeopardy, and his therefore pointless and brutal deed was almost certainly one of desperation – an act of weakness and sheer panic. Had he paused for one moment for thought he would have known that, even had he got away with it, it would still have changed nothing. Unlike Littleton, he did not have the luxury of being a pluralist with an alternative living, so shame, rejection, and ruin would have followed for him and his family.

It is also questionable whether he would have been allowed to remain in holy orders. At least he had the advantage of a good education, and his preaching talents might well have been in demand elsewhere, but it is debatable whether he would have ever found a way back into the Established Church. However, all this was never to be, and so must remain mere speculation.

For many years after his death Foulkes was not forgotten, because the story of his downfall continued to circulate in print well into the 18th-century, not least among sensational accounts of careers of other criminals, such as notorious murderers, robbers, highwaymen, and pirates. More significantly, however, his story found a place among anthologies of penitential literature, and in this regard it was unusual in that the writing was Foulkes' own, while the accounts of other penitents were perhaps for the most part the work of the Ordinaries of Newgate.

In 1690 John Dunton, the London bookseller and publisher, printed *The Wonders of Free-Grace: Or, A Compleat History of all the Remarkable Penitents That have been Executed at Tyburn, and elsewhere for these last Thirty Years*. This quoted extensively from Foulkes' *Alarme for Sinners*, and both his writing and his dignity at the end were very much held up as an inspirational model. Dunton, also the proprietor of the famous *Athenian Gazette: Or, Casuistical Mercury*, urged one of his more libidinous enquirers to read Foulkes' pamphlet, much recommending it 'to all secret Sinners for perusal', even thoughtfully informing him that it was 'printed for Langley Curtis on Ludgate-Hill'.[170]

Twenty years later Foulkes' writing surfaced again in the form of a flimsy penny chap-book. In 1708 a very slim ephemeral publication, on four leaves of thin paper, entitled *The Shropshire Amazement. Or, an Account of a Barbarous and Unnatural Murder committed by Mr. Robert Foulkes, Minister of Stanton Lacy* appeared on the London streets.[171] It was for the most part a verbatim reworking of Foulkes' *Alarme for Sinners*, from which it was almost entirely derived, it's main purpose, despite the misleading and sensational title, being to present the text in the form of a 'sermon'.

On the other hand some elements of the tale were by now becoming fanciful. Lacking a detailed account of the crime from his source, the writer concocted a brief introductory story clutching at whatever straws he could find in Foulkes' narrative. In want of a name for the woman, we learn here that his paramour was an orphan, one Sarah Floyd, who 'lived with him in the House, either as a servant, or Boarder'. Nor is there any mention of London, the infant apparently having been 'strangled' at Stanton Lacy. Where all this came from is anyone's guess, although it could well be a conflation with an account of some other crime. We are here witnessing the beginning of the transmutation of a story into something else, whether deliberately to serve a purpose, or by a natural process of degradation not unlike Chinese whispers. This was, however, by no means the last airing for Foulkes' writing, for the *Alarme* was yet again to see the light of day in 1804, when most of it was reprinted, in serialised form over four months, in *The Missionary Magazine*, an Edinburgh-based periodical.[172]

The object of this present book has been to try to dispel the fog of the passage of time, and to reassemble the scattered elements into a coherent and credible narrative.

Nevertheless, the revival of interest in a story can also be sparked off by a piece of creative writing, and rather more recently, in 1966, Foulkes put in a brief appearance in John Fowles' novel *The Magus*. The book's hero, Nicholas Urfe, is entertained on a Greek island by Conchis, the Magus, who hands him a copy of *An Alarme for Sinners*, recommending that he should read it. He notes its 'fine muscular pre-Dryden English', and that it is 'more real than any historical novel – more moving, more evocative, more human.'. Then, awakening later from a sleep in the garden, Nicholas becomes aware of a tableau being enacted before him as two figures in period dress, obviously Foulkes and his young mistress, come into view. They remain still, mute, staring at him from a distance, before they are absorbed back into the landscape as mysteriously as they had emerged, as if dissolving like phantasms back into the mists of time out of which they had materialized.

FINIS

Dramatis Personae

A number of interesting, even colourful, characters appear in this book. Some were major players in the plot, while others put in but a brief appearance and were only incidental to the main flow of the story. A few were but humble folk, and would otherwise have left little trace for the historian to find, beyond the barest facts of their existence from parish registers which, for most, is normally all that is left to show for an eventful life. These compact biographies of the significant players are merely designed for quick reference, and are intended to save readers having to search back through the text for information. Some additional facts have been included, in part to flesh out the little that is known, together with significant dates in their story. For ease of finding, they have been placed in alphabetical order. Dates are given in modern style, and all events took place at Stanton Lacy unless otherwise mentioned.

ANN ATKINSON (c.1650–)

Youngest child of Thomas Atkinson, vicar of Stanton Lacy, and Anne Whitmore, his second wife. Also known as 'Nan' Atkinson. Born in the parish in or about 1650, and since the age of fifteen said to have been very 'conversant' with Robert Foulkes. She inherited twenty pounds by the will of William Whitmore, her uncle and godfather, proved in November 1668. In 1673 she was sent to West Felton for six months to be delivered of her first illegitimate child by Foulkes, which was born in about May 1674. She returned to Stanton Lacy briefly before going to stay at Claverley with her uncle Thomas, and later in London with a 'kinsman'. In September 1674 she and Foulkes kept a tryst at the Talbot Inn in Worcester. She returned to Stanton Lacy at Christmas 1675, to find herself defrauded by William Hopton out of part of her inheritance. She was both a plaintiff and a witness at the Assize hearings in Shrewsbury against Hopton in August 1677. Her second child by Foulkes was conceived in early 1678, and delivered and murdered by him at York Buildings in the Strand on 11th December. Acquitted of murder at the Old Bailey on 16th January 1679, but remained in London for another three years. Returned to Stanton Lacy in the summer of 1682, when she was discharged by the consistory court. Possibly excommunicated following intercession by the archbishop of Canterbury, her subsequent fate is at present unknown.

ELIZABETH ATKINSON (c.1607–1689)

Born in about 1607 at Garnish, in the parish of Theydon Garnon in Essex, and perhaps related to Dr. Henry Withers, rector there between 1591 and 1609. Married Thomas Atkinson as his third wife in c.1654, and was widowed three years later. Stepmother of John, Francis, and Ann. After her husband she held the impropriation by lease of the rectoral tithe of Stanton Lacy township, also the lease of Hammonds Farm. Her brother's daughter, Mary Withers, eloped with William Hopton in c.1675. Elizabeth made three depositions in Foulkes'and Ann's defence. She made her last will in March 1682 during an illness, but survived for another seven years and was buried on the 27th June 1689.

FRANCIS ATKINSON (c.1648–1690)

Born at Stanton Lacy in about 1648, the second son of Thomas Atkinson and Anne Whitmore his second wife. Educated at Christ Church, Oxford. Matriculated May 1661, graduated there B.A. in February 1665, and M.A. from Trinity College, Cambridge in 1679. Curate at West Felton, Shropshire for seven years, during which Foulkes' and Ann's first child was delivered there, and baptized by Atkinson in

about May 1674. He was involved in making arrangements for the baby's maintenance; and later gave guarded evidence in 1677. Became rector of Wistanstow in May 1678, and also of Aston Botterell in September 1679. Buried at Wistanstow on 21st January 1690, after a sudden illness.

JOHN ATKINSON (1646–1697)
Physician. Born in Ludlow and baptized on 12th January 1646, the eldest son of Thomas Atkinson and Anne Whitmore his second wife. Educated at Christ Church, Oxford. Matriculated May 1661, and was at the Middle Temple in 1662. Made two depositions in 1677 in Foulkes' and Ann's defence. Married to Olive Davies, formerly Bowdler, the widow of a Ludlow apothecary, in November 1684 – he was her third husband. Atkinson died at Sarnesfield, Herefordshire, in September 1697, and was buried at Stanton Lacy on the 28th.

THOMAS ATKINSON (c.1604–1657)

Former vicar of Stanton Lacy. Born in about 1604. Graduated at Trinity College, Oxford, B.A in June 1626, M.A. in April 1629. Inducted as rector of Wistanstow in February 1639, and vicar of Stanton Lacy in May of the same year.
His first wife Anne died at Stanton Lacy in May 1642, having given him two sons who both died in infancy. He married Anne Whitmore of Claverley in about 1645, a cousin of his patron Lord Craven, who bore him three children, but she died in c.1650. Harrassed under the Commonwealth as a 'scandalous minister' in June 1651. Reinstated at Stanton Lacy by October 1651, but had been deprived of the rectory of Wistanstow. Married his third wife Elizabeth in about 1654. Died 8th April 1657 and was buried in the chancel, and is commemorated on an engraved brass plate.

SOMERSET BRABANT (1641–1682)

Inn attendant, peeping Tom, and Foulkes' nemesis. Born at Ludlow in early 1641, third son of John and Ann Brabant. By 1667 living in St. Michael in Bedwardine, Worcester. Apprenticed himself to William Barnard, a joiner and trunk maker, in St. Helen's, Worcester, in March 1667.  Married Anne Barnard seven months later, and by September 1674 was working as a chamberlain or room attendant at the Talbot Inn in Sydbury, close to Worcester cathedral. Witnessed a rendezvous between Foulkes and Ann at the inn when they stayed overnight. Attended the funeral of his father in August 1678 and, willingly or otherwise, was obliged to reveal what he had seen before Sir Timothy Baldwyn, the bishop's chancellor. Buried at St. Helen's, Worcester, on 14th April 1682.

DR. WILLIAM BRADLEY (c.1637–)

Rector of West Felton, and also of Stockton near Bridgnorth, where he lived. Born at Clapham, W. Yorkshire in about 1637. Doctor of Laws, and Judge or Official of the Royal Peculiar of Bridgnorth. Received  William Hopton when he visited West Felton unexpectedly in 1676 during his search for Foulkes' illegitimate child. Gave evidence in Foulkes' defence in February 1678. Dr. Bradley was also well acquainted with the Whitmores, who were his patrons. Dr. John Whitmore, who had died in July 1666, preceded Bradley as rector at both West Felton and Stockton, and was another of Francis and Ann Atkinson's uncles.

MARGARET CHEARME (c.1636–?1678)

Born at Middleton, in Bitterley parish, in about 1636, and married to Richard Chearme before 1666 when they had a daughter, Ann. She witnessed Foulkes and Ann Atkinson kissing and embracing at Hammonds Farm, and gave evidence in October 1676. Foulkes called her 'a lean scragg, all bones'.

She moved away with her husband in 1677, but may be the same as the Margaret Chearme buried at Bitterley in February 1678.

RICHARD CHEARME (1630–)

Yeoman farmer, baptized in High Ercall parish church on 10 January 1630. Lived at Burford, near Tenbury Wells, for six years before moving to Stanton Lacy in May 1674, becoming Elizabeth Atkinson's tenant at Hammonds Farm. Elected a churchwarden at Easter 1676, and with the encouragement of the Hoptons presented Foulkes before the bishop's court. Abused and struck by Foulkes with the fire tongs in July 1676, after which he became one of the six 'combinators'. Hutchinson judged him 'the most violent and bitter of them all'. He and his wife appear to have left Hammonds Farm in about May of 1677.

JOSEPH DOVEY 'THE ELDER' (c.1622–1682)

Yeoman farmer. Born in the parish of Quatt, near Bridgnorth, in around 1622. Arrived at Stanton Lacy in about 1668. Reputedly lived in a declared relationship with a widow, Martha Hawkes, to whom it was maintained he was not married because he had tried to obtain a marriage licence in Bridgnorth in 1674, after she had already formally sworn that she was his wife. Dovey joined the 'combinators' supposedly in revenge for Foulkes having previously promoted or encouraged a lawsuit against Martha, brought by Ralph, Lord Eure . He was buried at Stanton Lacy on the 11th February 1682.

MARTHA DOVEY (1632–1696)

Supposed wife of Joseph Dovey, the elder. Martha, the daughter of Daniel Cage, was baptized in the parish church of Lindsey, in Suffolk, on the 17th June 1632. She was also neice to Lady Martha Eure, her father's sister, who was widow of the eminent lawyer Sir Sampson Eure. As Martha 'Gage' she married a John Hawkes at Stanton Lacy in July 1653, but was widowed in July

1666. Swore an affidavit in c.1670 to the effect that she had married Joseph Dovey. There were doubts when she was later sued for debt by Ralph, Lord Eure, with the support of Robert Foulkes, as a 'feme sole' or woman of independent means, which she did not deny. In 1676 she was named as one of the 'combinators' in the case against Foulkes, and gave evidence in October, her visits to Elizabeth Atkinson's house giving her the chance to observe Foulkes' and Ann's uninhibited familiarity together. In March 1678 she was presented for rowdy behaviour in church during services. She was buried as Martha Dovey, widow, on the 4th September 1696.

RALPH FENTON (1627–1685)
Rector of Ludlow. Born at Fenton, Stoke on Trent, in 1627. Matriculated at All Souls College, Oxford, July 1642. Inducted Rector at Ludlow in about 1658, then also appointed Preacher of Ludlow in 1661. Sat as the chancellor's deputy during the court proceedings, also giving evidence as a character witness in Foulkes' defence. Buried at Ludlow 8th May 1685.

ISABELLA FOULKES (1634–)

Baptized Isabella Colbatch at Ludlow, 20th February 1634, daughter of Thomas Colbatch, rector of Ludlow, and Mary his wife. Her father died in October 1637. Spent her adolescence in the Atkinson household at Stanton Lacy, before her marriage to Robert Foulkes on the 7th September 1657. She was the mother of four children by Foulkes, a girl and three boys. On discovering her husband's illegitimate child, she was said to have forged letters in aid of William Hopton's fraudulent attempt to transfer leases to Mary Withers. Abused and beaten by Foulkes when the story of his affair became public knowledge. Called as a witness at Shrewsbury Assizes in August 1677. After Foulkes' execution, Isabella complained to Sir Timothy Baldwyn about Ann Atkinson's apparent immunity from prosecution. Upon

Ann's discharge by the consistory court, in 1682 she approached the Bishop of St. Asaph, Dr. William Lloyd, who wrote to the Archbishop of Canterbury. The subsequent fate of Isabella and her children is at present uncertain.

ROBERT FOULKES (1634–1679)

A Welshman, and the subject of our story. Baptized on the 19th March 1634 at Mallwyd in Montgomeryshire. Admitted a scholar at the Royal Free School in Shrewsbury in 1648/49; and as a servitor at Christ Church, Oxford, from the autumn of 1651, where he matriculated in November 1652. After four years of tuition he became a preacher, and married Isabella Colbatch at Ludlow on the 7th September 1657, by whom he later had four children. Presented to Stanton Lacy parish church in May 1660, and inducted there as vicar in the following September at the age of 26. After years of apparent respectability, he became emotionally involved with Ann Atkinson, daughter of the previous vicar, and a girl child was born in about May 1674. Presented before the consistory court in August 1676 by parishioners for his scandalous misbehaviour, followed by two years of litigation. Took Ann Atkinson to London in the autumn of 1678, where he delivered and murdered their second illegitimate child on the 11th December, at York Buildings in the Strand. Sentenced to death at the Old Bailey 16th January 1679, and hanged at Tyburn on the 31st following. Author of *An Alarme for Sinners*, published in 1679.

MARTHA HAWKES, see Martha Dovey

MARY HOPTON, see Mary Withers

RICHARD HOPTON, SENIOR (1621–1690)

Son of a George Hopton. Baptized the 29th December 1621, and father of Richard junior and William. He served as a churchwarden on at least seven occasions between 1651 and 1673; and was said to have misappropriated £10, part of the parish poor fund that he held in trust, claiming to have placed it in the hands of a former churchwarden, John Knight, who was now dead. Hopton pretended to sue Knight's widow for the money, but she affirmed it had already been repaid long before. Foulkes publicly rebuked Hopton from the pulpit, earning his evident resentment. Although not directly involved as a 'combinator', in June 1678, following his son William's departure, he obtained a warrant from a justice of the peace to make further enquiries at West Felton about the birth of Foulkes' first illegitimate child. Hopton was buried on the 25th July 1690.

RICHARD HOPTON, JUNIOR (1642–1715)

Eldest surviving son of Richard Hopton senior; baptized the 10th November 1642. His second wife was Hannah, the daughter of a Nicholas Tippen. Her father approached Foulkes to speak to his son-in-law and counsel him to withdraw from a bond that guaranteed William Hopton's honest conduct in acting as a bailiff to Lord Craven. This antagonised all the Hoptons, who resented Foulkes' interference, and Richard Hopton was later named as one of the 'combinators'. He was buried in February 1715.

WILLIAM HOPTON (c.1651–   )

Second surviving son of Richard Hopton, senior; born in about 1651. Plainly the least affable of the Hoptons, and had spent time in London where he had an illegitimate child with 'a coffy mans maid' near Gray's Inn. Becoming a bailiff to Lord Craven, he greatly resented Foulkes' interference concerning a bond to pledge his good conduct, and thereafter sought revenge.

Foulkes' affair with Ann Atkinson not only gave him the opportunity to discredit his vicar, but he attempted to defraud Ann out of part of her inheritance in favour of

Mary Withers, Elizabeth Atkinson's niece, whom he then married in around 1675. At around the same time he became an innkeeper in Stanton Lacy; and actively sought evidence about Foulkes' and Ann's illegitimate child, visiting West Felton and Llansantffraid in June 1676, and becoming the most vociferous of the 'combinators'. After intercepting legal documents in the care of a Ludlow carrier, he was prosecuted at the Shrewsbury Assizes in August 1677. He thereafter absconded, allegedly with £1000 of Lord Craven's money, and is not heard of again. The case against Foulkes subsequently almost collapsed.

FRANCIS HUTCHINSON, alias Hutchenson, Hitchinson etc. Yeoman farmer, and a cousin to William and Richard Hopton. Moved to Stanton Lacy 'from a distant place' in about June 1676, some six weeks before he was 'inveigled' by the Hoptons into acting as 'promoter' in their case against Foulkes. Signed additional articles for the prosecution in November 1676. After William Hopton's disappearance in 1678, he withdrew as promoter saying that he had been a total stranger to Foulkes, and had known nothing ill of him. He appears to have moved away from Stanton Lacy not long after.

LUKE MILNER (c.1627–1683)
Butcher, of High Street, Bridgnorth. Born c.1627 in Bridgnorth. Approached by Joseph Dovey in 1674, who came into his shop and asked him to support his application for a marriage licence from Dr. Bradley. He refused, because Dovey would not divulge the identity of his proposed wife. Gave evidence in September 1677 in support of Foulkes' case by discrediting Dovey. 'Mr. Millner' was buried at St. Leonard's church, Bridgnorth, on the 29th August 1683.

CHARLES PEARCE (1637–1690)
Farmer, of East Fields in Stanton Lacy. Born in the parish, where he had lived for most of his life. Accompanied William

Hopton on his journey to Whittington and West Felton in June 1676, and claimed to have seen Foulkes' child at Llansantffraid where he obtained a lock of her hair. With Mary his wife he was presented before the bishop's court for slander in December 1676. Pearce was also present with Richard Hopton senior during the interrogation of witnesses before Robert Owen, a Justice of the Peace, at West Felton in June 1678. He was buried on the 30th October 1690.

JOHN SLADE (c.1644–1721)

Vicar of Bromfield from 1669. Stated he was born in the parish of Onibury in c.1644, although there is no trace of his baptism in the register. Gave evidence before the court in February 1677, having assisted at Stanton Lacy by taking services and preaching. The year before, at the widow Partridge's alehouse on Old Field, he gave advice to Foulkes, which he said was received 'very kindly and quietly', although in private Foulkes was furious. In 1678 Slade became rector of Kingsland, Herefordshire, and then prebendary of Norton in Hereford cathedral in 1684. He died in February 1721.

EDWARD SMALMAN (c.1643–1718)

Attorney, born at Kinnersley, Shropshire, in about 1643. His family appear to have had Ludlow connections since before the Civil War. He settled in Ludlow in 1670, marrying an Anne Hawlyn by licence in September 1671; and by the following year was living at 55 Broad Street. Professionally he acted for Foulkes when he sued William Hopton and Richard Chearme, and he was also involved in other litigation on behalf of the Atkinsons. He lodged with Foulkes at the Fox Inn in Shrewsbury during the Assizes in August 1677. Smalman later served for nearly twenty years as town clerk of Ludlow; and he became related through marriage to the Atkinsons when Olive, the widow of his cousin Edward Davies the apothecary, later married John Atkinson the physician in November 1684. Smalman had at least four children by his first wife, who died in 1700, and a daughter by his second wife, Catherine. He was buried on the 30th August 1718.

FRANCIS UNDERWOOD (?1617–1690)

He is probably the Francis Underwood baptized at the parish church in November 1617. We never hear his voice in testimony, but he was drawn into the story on several occasions. We are told that he occupied a house as Ann Atkinson's tenant, and after the birth of her first child in May 1674, she spent about a month there recuperating. Underwood and his second wife, Judith, were invited to the vicarage for supper in July 1676, but managed to leave before Foulkes became violent. Not long afterwards Foulkes and Ann regularly used their house for assignations, on one occasion being surrounded by watchers who taunted Foulkes as he left, and later Underwood was sent in vain to the alehouse in the hope it would draw William Hopton away. He was buried on the 24th May 1690.

THOMAS WHITMORE (1599–1677)

The eldest brother of Anne Whitmore, mother to the three children of Thomas Atkinson, and the then-head of the Whitmore family of Ludstone Hall. He was a lawyer, becoming a barrister-at-law at the Middle Temple in 1626, and a bencher in 1648. In 1659/60 he was Recorder and M.P. for Much Wenlock. During the summer of 1674 Ann Atkinson evidently stayed with him for a time at Ludstone, and Richard Hopton senior claimed to have informed him of the existence of her first child. He was buried at Claverley on the 30th May 1677, but there is no mention of any of the Atkinsons in his will.[173]

WILLIAM WHITMORE (1603–1668)

William Whitmore's voice is not heard in the court documents, for he was long dead by the commencement of the litigation. He was the second eldest brother of Anne Whitmore, mother to the three children of Thomas Atkinson, and lived at Shipley in the parish of Claverley. He was named in Atkinson's will in

1657 as their uncle and guardian. In his own will, made on Boxing Day 1667, he left twenty shillings to his 'Sister in Law Mistress Atkinson for to buy her a Ringe'; five pounds apiece to his nephews John and Francis; 'And I doe give and bequeath to my Neece and God daughter Anne Atkinson the summe of Twenty pounds'. He was buried at Claverley on the 27th June 1668, and his will proved in the following November.[174]

MARY WITHERS (1655–   )

Daughter of a John Withers, who was described by Elizabeth Atkinson as her 'brother', although this term was used more loosely for a brother-in-law. Mary was born at Standlake in Oxfordshire on 10th February 1655. Came to live with her aunt Elizabeth at Hammond's Farm in about 1664. At the age of about 20 she eloped with William Hopton, having colluded in defrauding Ann Atkinson of part of her inheritance during her absence. As Mary Hopton, she gave evidence to the court in October 1676. Possibly abandoned by Hopton when he disappeared in 1677, but she was a beneficiary of Elizabeth's will made in 1682.

JOAN WOOD (1653–   )

Born in 1653. The daughter of Edward Wood of Walton, Onibury, with whom she lived, her mother having died two years before. Employed as a maid servant in the Foulkes household for about seven weeks, during June and July 1676. She became involved when she twice came running out of the vicarage to summon help for Isabella Foulkes, who was being beaten up by her husband. Foulkes dismissed her soon after, he said, because she and her sister had become too friendly with William Hopton.

Appendix

Following their abolition during the Commonwealth, the diocesan consistory courts had been restored in 1661, and were particularly active during the next decade or so. Nevertheless, by the end of the 17th-century they had significantly declined, partly because of competition with civil courts, and partly on account of their great unpopularity. The process was not only expensive and slow, but because of the nature of their concerns the courts were seen as both oppressive and corrupt.

Two sorts of business were conducted – Acts of Office, and Acts of Instance. In the first, the consistory court prosecuted offences that were contrary to canon law and, where it had authority, also contrary to statute. In this correctional function, the court punished offences such as failing to attend church, whether as a dissenter, a catholic or recusant, or one who was irreligious; the commission of moral misdemeanours like fornication before marriage, adultery, or incest; or blasphemy, and bad behaviour in church.

The courts also prosecuted the clergy for neglect of their cure, moral lapses, or conducting illegal or 'clandestine' marriages; also midwives or schoolteachers who practiced without a licence. Most of these cases were 'presented' by churchwardens, because it was part of their statutory duty to do so, but not surprisingly churchwardens became increasingly reluctant to present their friends and neighbours. The judge, that is the 'Chancellor' of the diocese, or his deputy, summarily heard the cases, questioned the defendants and witnesses orally, and fined offenders.

Failure to attend the court, which was increasingly common, could be punished by excommunication – an ultimate sanction, in that it denied you Christian burial.

The Acts of Instance were the other facet of the court's business, and they were recorded in separate books. These were cases brought at the 'instance' of private individuals against others, both clergy and laymen. Here the clergy would sue for non-payment of tithes or other fees; and private suits would be brought for defamation, or disputes over marriage and wills, or squabbles over church pews. These took time and generated large amounts of paperwork, and were a lucrative source of income for the lawyers and other court officials.

The Foulkes case, however, was one that fell between two stools, in that it was a disciplinary case against a member of the clergy, and yet it was a private individual or 'promoter' who brought the action. These 'Promoted Office' causes were a means of allowing the laity to bring a prosecution when the church authorities might have hesitated in acting for themselves. They were also a means of getting private individuals to fund the proceedings, rather than doing so at the cost of the diocese.

Where surviving, it is the paperwork that these cases generated that is the invaluable historical resource. Of all late 17th-century documents available to the local historian, the depositions submitted before the consistory courts are, as regards social history, certainly some of the most revealing. A typical deposition usually starts mundanely enough with the witness's name; parish of residence; occupation; how long he or she had lived there; the parish of birth if different; and his or her age, which was frequently an approximation and could even vary with successive statements. Just this biographical detail in itself can be particularly useful, for it provides information about individuals of low estate that would usually be hard to come by from other sources. Some of the terminology used in these documents may need a little explanation. Charges or allegations were termed 'libels' by the defence, and were divided under subject headings or 'articles'. People, things, or events mentioned in 'articles' were described as being 'articulate'. The accusations would be replied to by the defendant, in article order, in a series of 'responsa'; and any counter-charges or questioning were termed 'interrogata'. Witnesses who supported one side or the other made written 'depositions', and were therefore 'deponents'. In the same document, after their statements and when they were subject to questioning, they then became 'respondents'.

The Court Books, where a memorandum of witnesses questioned was kept, and the progress of the hearings summarised, were for the most part written by the registrar in Latin, although accusations and answers originally given in English were usually quoted as such. Subsequent notes, questions, and answers were in Latin; as were points of law made between the lawyers, and any private discussions conducted in open court, so as to be incomprehensible to those without the education to understand the language.

On the other hand, witnesses' depositions, usually in English, are often remarkable in that they record the language, activities, and attitudes of a cross-section of society rarely obtained from other documents. Parish registers simply record the dates of the most significant events in individuals' lives, and brief biographical detail is very rare.

Wills tell us about relationships and possessions, but tend to be of people of higher status who had property to bequeath. While these folk also frequently figure in consistory court documents, depositions often reveal the day-to-day activities of the most humble stratum of society, whose voice is rarely heard in other sources.

Here the uncensored everyday speech of ordinary people comes vividly to life, coarse wit and sharp unguarded reposts said in the heat of a moment fly about, and the results to our ears can be frequently hilarious. This was particularly so where the vulgar, scandalous or seditious language uttered was part of the key evidence in a prosecution.

Despite their formal and formulaic style as official documents, for they were after all drafted by lawyers, of whose hovering presence in the background we need to remain aware, the vernacular and figures of speech of real people still shine through. Nonetheless this formal style can be a little cumbersome and tedious to read, if all the reader wants is the plain essence of what was actually said.

For the purposes of this book, therefore, much of the repetitive wording, which was inserted in the interests of supposed legal precision, can be safely stripped away. The result is that a sentence such as: 'And further the said Ann Rogers deposed that she was present when the articulate Ann Atkinson was in labour & saw the said Ann delivered & the said child taken from her body' has been rendered as: 'And further Ann Rogers deposed that she was present when Ann Atkinson was in labour, & saw her delivered, & the child taken from her body'. This loses none of the essence of the original, and provides a more readable text that is far closer to the words actually spoken by the deponent.

Punctuation, practically non-existent in the original, has been inserted where it helps to divide up clauses in the text, but the former spelling has been retained to give some flavour of the original.

DOCUMENT 1

The National Archives: ref. Prob. 11/273, ff.188v/189r

Will of Thomas Atkinson
dated 6 April 1657

In the name of God Amen, forasmuch as every Christian Soule groaneing under the burden of the earthlie Tabernacle is subject to dissolucion, and that in this world wee have noe continueing Citty, I Thomas Atkinson Clearke being sicke in body but of good and perfect memorie praised be God doe make constitute and ordeyne this my last will and Testament in manner and forme followeing **First** (as every good Christian ought) I give and bequeath my soule into the hands of God my Creator, hopeing by the meritts of Jesus Christ my redeemer and through faith in his blood to be made partaker of Eternall blisse, And my body to be buried in the Chancell of Stannton Lacy by my former wiefe **Item** I give and bequeath unto my Deare wife Mistress Elizabeth Atkinson all my personall estate (save that which is hereafter excepted) desiring her to be carefull of my daughter Ann in A speciall manner, And to add what she pleases towards her porcion **Item** I give and bequeath to my sonne John when he shall attaine to the Age of twenty one yeares the farme of Withy poole, in the meane tyme my will is that the rent of that Farme should goe towards the mayntenance of all my Children. **Item** I give and bequeath to my sonn Francis the howse and liveing wherein I now live after his mothers decease; **Item** I give and bequeath to my daughter Ann the Lease of the Tithes of Stanton Lacy after my wiefs decease. **Item** I give and bequeath to my brother Mr William Whitmore the choice of what horse or mare hee is pleased to make choice of. **Item** I leave the care and charge of the tuition of my children to my wiefe and their Uncle William Whitmore. **Item** I give and bequeath to Mr Whittell for preaching my funerall sermon and for his paynes with me in my siknes the some of Fifty shillings **Item** I give & bequeath [fo.189r] Unto my old servant Elizabeth Floyd twenty shillings **Item** I give and bequeath to my servant Edward Knolls Five pounds. **Item** I give and bequeath to my maid Rebecca twenty shillings. **Item** I give and bequeath to Andrew and John Falconer, and Henry [?] Tenn Shillings a peece. **Item** I give to my other servants the two men and the two mayds five shillings a peece. **Item** I give and bequeath to Francis Walker the sonne of Mr Richard Walker the young Graie mare called Cotte; **Item** I give and bequeath to the poore of the parish of Stanton Lacy five pounds to be paid in within a twelve month this to be towards the publique Stock; **Item** I doe make my deare wiefe Mistress Elizabeth Atkinson my sole Executrix, and I doe revoke all former Wills by me heretofore made, Witnes my hand and seale the sixt day of Aprill in the yeare of our Lord God One thowsand six hundred fifty seaven. Sealed and delivered in presence of William Pickering; Jenkin Jones; Mary Colbach, William Whittell Clerke.

This Will was proved at **London** before the Judges for probate of wills &c this Five and twentieth day of February English Stile One thowsand six hundred fifty seaven by the oath of Elizabeth Atkinson the relict and executrix &c To whom Administracion was Committed she being first sworne by Commission truely to administer.

Herefordshire Record Office: ref. HD4/25

Consistory Court Papers: 1675–76

The presentment of Richard Churme Churchwarden of the parish of Stannton Lacy made this 29th day of August 1676, to ye Right worshipfull Sir Timothy Baldwyn Chancellor of ye diocesse of Hereford

Inprimis I present Mr Robert Foulkes Clerke vicar of Staunton for neglectinge his duty and absentinge himselfe from the Church and leaveinge it destitute of divine service for some Sundayes within this yeare last past and for neglectinge to instruct the youth in the Church Caterchisme for theise two yeares last past, hee is a very Contentious man and doth make it his great busines to sett his neighbours att variance one with annother, hee is vehemently suspected for liveinge incontinently with one Anne Atkinson of the parish aforesaid, and of the same there is a Common & publique voyce fame & reporte within the parish of Staunton Lacy & other adjacent parishes. hee is very disorderly and scandalous in his life and Conversacion, and doth suffer his house and barnes to goe out of repaire.

[In Latin] Exhibited before me the day and year aforesaid his mark Richard R Churme

Herefordshire Record Office: at reference HD4/26

Consistory Court Papers: 1676–79

Office of the Lord Bishop, promoted through Cornwall, against Foulkes. Allegations on behalf of Foulkes, exhibited 26th February 1677/78; Hutchinson's Affidavit (a transcript included in a longer defence document)

I, Francis Hutchenson, of the parish of Staunton Lacy in the County of Salop, yeoman, doe voluntarily and of my owne accord and free mocion desire that for the manifestacion of the truth I may be admitted upon my oath to make and leave in writinge an attestacion of my knowledge in a matter wherein I have beene made playntiff or promoter in a cause now or lately dependinge in the Chancellors courte, against Robert Foulkes, Clerke, defendant. And beinge soe admitted to my oath I doe depose and acknowledge that at the first promocion of those articles against the sayd Robert Foulkes, I was a strainger both to the person and the accions of Mr Foulkes, and that I did not then nor doe I yet know any harme or evill of him, but I was instigated and inviegled thereinto by the importunate sollicitacion of other persons who were then, and (as I believe) are yet, malliciously bent against Mr Foulkes, in particular by William Hopton of Staunton Lacy, ale seller, and Richard Hopton junior, his brother (both my relacions). These Hoptons to perswade mee against Mr Foulkes told mee they had five or six goode stakes in the hedge, meaninge thereby five or six able and substantiall persons who would stick to mee in the managinge of that suite against Mr Foulkes, beare all the charges of it, defende and indemnify mee from all advantages that Mr Foulkes might have against mee for and by reason of the said prosecucion. The Stakes or persons concerned were (as William Hopton informed mee) himselfe the said William, and Richard his brother, Richard Chearme, Joseph Dovey the elder and Martha his wife, all of Staunton Lacy aforesayd; and allsoe, as the same informacion tells mee, Richard Wreddenhall of Dounton in the sayd parish, gentleman, and for these reasons I think in my conscience that the sayd Wreddenhall was concerned in combinacion against Mr Foulkes because he frequented the company and meetinges of the rest of the combinators, had private whisperinge and conference with them, and directed (as I was informed) how and by whom the articles should be put in against Mr Foulkes, tellinge them (as I was informed by William Hopton) that if they became promotors themselves (which they intended) they would loose theyre evidence, to preserve which Wreddenhall told them they must provide a promotor that had little or nothinge to say, and then themselves might become wittnesses. And thereupon they sollicited mee, and I out of ignorance complyed with them, and the rather because I was perswaded by Mr Cornwall theyre proctor soe to doe, who tolde mee it was but deliveringe in a paper which (he sayd) any body might doe without danger. This Mr Cornwall aforesayd I never retayned nor gave any money to but fifty shillinges, which Cornwall sent me for to William Hopton, which Hopton allsoe received from Richard Chearme, and I from him, and soe delivered it Mr Cornwall. And since the sayd William Hopton for his misscariages was forced to leave his Country, I am informed by Mary his wife and Martha Dovey that Mr Cornwall was payd the charges of that suite by William Hopton and the rest of the combinators, all within tenne or twenty shillinges. I doe allsoe depose that in the courte before Croft Castle I did see the aforesayd persons the combinators makinge a purse, as they called it, and each of them in particular givinge his share of money to William Hopton, who was to give it to a servant of my lord bishops, which servant was to introduce the combinators to his lordship, and as much as could be to stand theyre secret freinde to his lordship. I declare and depose that the articles were never wholy reade to mee, nor did I know what was contained in some of them, or give any direcion aboute the draught or prosecucion of them, that was done (I conceave) in my absence by the combinators at Brimfield Crosse, and from time to time at Ludlow or other places of theyre meetinges, where Mr Wreddenhall frequently mett them upon court dayes and did enquire what success they had. I doe allsoe declare and depose that upon the 30th day of October last, beinge the Chancellors court day, Mr Cornwall did solliscit mee to proceede in my prosecution against Mr Foulkes, and to engage mee therein tolde mee that if I did not proceede, Mr Foulkes would have charges against me, but if I went on it should cost me nothing, or wordes to that effect. I doe allsoe declare and depose that lately, in the house of William Hopton in Staunton Lacy, Richard Chearme did perswade me to goe as himselfe did in the law against Mr Foulkes, or, in case I would not, then he the sayd Chearme desired mee to make as little use or mencion of his name as could be, meaninge thereby (as I conceaved) that I should not confesse him to be one of the combinators, allthough I judge him to be the most violent and bitter of them all.

Francis Hutchinson

Sworn at Ludlow in the County of Salop on the 12th day of November in the 29th Year of King Charles the Second [1677] before me, Thomas Crumpe, Master in Chancery Extraordinary.

DOCUMENT 4

Testimony of Somerset Brabant
21 August 1678

Herefordshire Record Office: at reference HD4/26
Consistory Court Papers: 1676/79

Office of the Lord Bishop, promoted through Cornwall, against
Foulkes

[In Latin] Testimony examined 21st August 1678, of Somerset
Brabant of the parish of St. Helen's in the City of Worcester,
joiner, where he has lived for the space of 12 years last past or
thereabouts, born in the parish of Ludlow in the County of
Salop, and aged 42 [in fact he was 37] years or thereabouts,
testimony produced sworn and examined, deposeth and saith
as follows viz:

...That about Michaelmas 4 years since [i.e. end of September
1674] or thereabouts to this deponents best remembrance Ann
Atkinson came unto the house of Mistress Bridget Walker at
the sign of the Talbott in Sydbury within the City of Worcester,
where this deponent was and still is a chamberlain, and with her
a maid servant of the Lady Craven's, where Mr Robert Foulks,
clerke, the party against whom this business is promoted
met them, and calling for a chamber was directed unto one
that was next adjoyning unto that wherein Ann was, and he
enquired for the said Ann, whereupon she went immediately
unto him: and then Robert bespoak a supper, and whilst it was
provideing they continued alone in the said Roberts chamber,
and this deponent goeing somtimes into the same chamber, and
very well knowing them both, observed much intimacy and

familiarity betwixt them, as kissing, hugging, and embraceing each other after such a manner as made this deponent suspect that they had some further intention, especially seeing the bedd in the same chamber very much tumbled.

And thereupon this deponent, pulling off his shoes that he might not be heard or discovered, went into another chamber of the house, adjoyning alsoe to that wherein Robert and Ann were; and looking through a lardg hole in the wall divideing both chambers, and with his hand turning aside the hangings, did see Robert and Ann togeather upon the aforesaid bedd, and Robert upon the bare belly of Ann stirring and labouring as in the very act of uncleaness, after which manner they continued near the space of a quarter of an hower, whilst this deponent plainly saw Anns cloths up, with her leggs spread abroad and her thighes bare and naked, and Robert betwixt them labouring as before.

And this deponent alsoe saw Robert rise off Ann, she putting down her coats and he thrusting his member with his hand into his breeches, and when they had sate a little while in the same chamber at a small distance each from other, Robert ledd Ann againe to the bedd, and lifting her there upon pulled up her clothes and cast himself upon her naked belly betwixt her leggs and thighes, which this deponent saw naked and bare, and there he continued about the same space of time as before, labouring as in the very act of adultery or fornicacion, and this deponent afterwards saw them come off the said bedd, shee putting down her clothes and he setting up his member as this deponent beleeveth, and then sitting down near each other by the bedd side they wept to each other about a quarter of an hower without speaking any thing as this deponent heard.

And this deponent verily beleeveth in his conscience for the reasons aforesaid that Robert at both those times had the carnall knowledge of the body of Ann, and did perpetrate act and committ adultery or fornicacion with her. And then the table being laid and supper brought up, they did eate and drink togeather, and were very pleasant and merry all supper time, whilst this deponent attended upon them, and still observed their more then ordinary familiarity.

And after supper this deponent left them togeather alone in the same chamber, but still suspecting that they would goe againe to their base accions, this deponent went as before privately and quietly to the aforesaid hole, and looking through the same as before plainly saw Robert sitting in a chaire near unto the fire, which gave a great light in the same room, and haveing first put out the candle took Ann betwixt his leggs and pulled up her coats, and putting his arms about her embraced her as close as possibly he could, with their faces towards each other, kissing and clipping with much vigour and earnestness for about the space of 2 houres at the least, dureing which Ann smileing upon Robert would often say 'Fie Fie for God sake be quiet, doe [?you] think this is handsom', but never strived or endeavoured to get from betwixt his leggs.

However, to make the maid, which stayed for her in the chamber where they intended to lye, beleeve that she was coming to her, as this deponent conceived, Ann did severall times with a loud voice cry 'Good night, good night'. [And further this deponent says] that Ann continued between Roberts leggs in manner as aforesaid untill about 12 of the clock in the night, and immediately before they departed she earnestly begged of Robert that he would never discover what had passed betwixt them at that time, which he promised he would never doe, but she told him that she would not beleeve unless he would swear soe much to her, whereupon they, kneeling down togeather upon the hearth before the fire, solemnly vowed and mutually protested to each other that they would never discover what was then donn betwixt them.

And soe kissing each other they parted, she goeing to her chamber, and he staying in his. [In answer to further questioning, this deponent says that] he was told by the maid, which came togeather and lay with Ann, that the next morning Robert came into the chamber where Ann was in bedd with the maid, and thrust his hand into the bedd and felt Ann's naked thighes and other parts of her body, and that he endeavoured to touch or feel the maid, which made her leap out of the bedd and leave them togeather, whilst she dressed herself in the same chamber. [Beyond this he has nothing further to say] saveing that Robert dischardged the whole reckoning, and this deponent beleeveth that Ann had noe other business in Worcester at that time then to meet Robert, and that neither of them had or has been at the aforesaid house before or since, and this deponent hath heard and beleeveth that they were intimate and familiar togeather at the Crown and other places in the City of Worcester.

Jonmarshal Brabant

DOCUMENT 5

Herefordshire Record Office: at reference HD7/20/355
(Diocesan Registrars Files)

It is this day ordered by Sir Timothy Baldwyn
Chancellor that the Churchwardens of the parish
of Ludlow are required not to permitt Mr Robert
Foulks vicar of Staunton Lacy to preach in the
Parish Church of Ludlow aforesaid till they have
further orders from the Lord Bishopp of this diocese
or the said Chancellor

Dated 20th August 1678
[signed]

Hen. Haynes, Notary Public

Let a Coppy of this order under the Register or his
deputy his hand bee forth with sent to the Churchwardens
of Ludlow and to Mr Fenton

DOCUMENT 6

Robert Foulkes' last words spoken at the place of execution

Tyburn, 31st January 1679

Good Christian People:

I intend not, and I hope you will not expect any long Discourse at this time; but I have taken care that my Confession, wherein (as I shall by and by answer to the God of Truth) you will finde nothing but the truth, shall be published more fully, and to your better advantage, than I could possibly make it here. In a few words therefore:

You may in me see what sin is, and what it will end in: you may in me see the lamentable and irreparable mischiefs of Uncleanness and Hypocrisie in particular; and what it is for one who was a Member of Christ, to make himself a Member of a Harlot. It is a sin that seldome goes single and alone: it is the Mother-sin to abundance more, and they more ugly and deformed than it self: I have found it by sad and woeful experience. It led me to Lying, to Oaths and Execrations, to conceal and defend it: Nay, I went further, to advise, contrive, and assist in what might procure Abortions; which certainly, in the sight of God, was Murther in intention. Nor stopt it there, but went forward to murther in Act and Execution: for which crying sin I am come hither to satisfie the Law of man, and do acknowledge the Justice of that Sentence.

And Oh that all you may fear and tremble at God's holy and righteous Judgements, which have overtaken me; and that they may make you take warning to avoid the snares of a whorish woman, and especially to keep the Married bed undefiled.

Beware of hypocritical pretences to religion, of coming to the Holy Sacrament while you live in these practices. Do not grieve or quench the Holy Spirit of God, nor stifle the Convictions of your own Consciences, lest God leave you (as he did me) to work all Uncleanness with greediness; and lest at last you be brought to this most miserable condition to which he has most justly brought me, to whose most righteous Judgement I do submit. I forgive all the world, as I desire to find mercy at God's hands through Jesus Christ. I do earnestly desire you, by me to take warning not to continue in sin, for in the end it will finde you out.

As to my sin, I have but two things to say: one I have cause exceedingly to lament, and that is, the great Scandal I have thereby brought upon Religion, and the holy Function of the Ministery. The great disparagement which reflects on these, I look upon as the most hainous Aggravation of my loose and licentious life: Therefore I pray you take up no prejudices against them upon my Account: they are holy and good, and grant no Licenses at all to such wicked and ungodly practices as I have been guilty of.

The other I have some reason to rejoyce in: 'Tis true, my sin has exposed the whole Nation to Judgement, for 'through Blood the Land is defiled'; but this is my comfort, that God by this punishment makes me expiate that Guilt, for the Judgement falls upon my own pate; and I hope through the mercy of God, and merit of Christ, will proceed no further than my body. I desire all that hear me, to take warning, not to continue in sin, but betimes to 'cease to do evil, and learn to do well.'

Now the Lord be with you all, and have mercy upon my poor Soul; for which I desire you to pray with me and for me to the last moment of my life.

DOCUMENTS 7 & 8

Reprinted next are two contemporary printed tracts, copies of which are now extremely rare.

The first is entitled: *A true and perfect Relation of the Tryal and Condemnation, Execution and last Speech of that unfortunate Gentleman Mr. Robert Foulks* ... London: Printed for L. White in White-cross street, 1679. It was one of a large number of slim ephemeral publications, hastily compiled and churned out weekly by printing presses across London, designed to satisfy the intense interest of the general public in religious issues and current events. Tracts like this were the progenitors of the first true newspapers, and these indeed were to appear within a very few years. Like much tabloid journalism today, the accuracy of the contents of many of these pamphlets is questionable, and this one is no exception.

The text starts off with a short account of the activities and execution of two catholics, William Ireland and John Grove, who were caught up in the mass-hysteria of what is referred to as 'the late Hellish Plot' – or Popish Plot. It includes a very brief but graphic description of their execution that, in the light of historical fact, appears to have been fanciful nonsense, written more to fulfil the expectations of an over-excited public, and the morbid gratification of the readership.

In the text, Ireland and Grove are given a typical traitor's execution in first being hanged, then 'cut down whilst some life remained in them', before being eviscerated. In fact, according to Professor Kenyon, the king had given specific instructions that Ireland and Grove were to be hanged until dead, and *not* disembowelled.[175] Nonetheless, the account of Foulkes' trial and execution seems accurate enough, although it does refer to Stanton Lacy as Stanton Hay; and the version of his final speech from the gallows appears to have been largely improvised before the true text, as printed in *An Alarme for Sinners*, became available. Despite the writer claiming to have been present, he appears to have heard very little, and what is printed in default of the real thing seems more his idea of what he thought ought to have been said, if not also what he thought his readership would have expected to hear.

The second tract is *The Execution of Mr. Rob. Foulks, late Minister of Stanton-Lacy in Shropshire...* London: Printed for R.G. 1679. It too was printed a few days before *An Alarme for Sinners* went to press, but the writer obviously knew about Foulkes' papers, and what was being prepared for publication. The identity of R.G. is unknown but he was very probably the author, and his turn of phrase and working knowledge of Latin suggests that he might have been a member of the clergy. The short text is in part a stout defence of the Church, and he asks that the reader should not judge the institution by the actions of one man, quoting the proverb: *Crimine ab uno disce omnes* (From the guilt of one learn the character of all). This, he says, 'is but Poetical Logick', and therefore scarcely appropriate in the case a black sheep. Against the backdrop of history, and the mass hysteria surrounding the period of the Popish Plot, this squalid yet tragic little murder may well seem to have been a minor happening of little relevance or significance. Nonetheless, at the time, the Church clearly viewed it with some gravity, fearing that a spark might be fanned into something rather more serious, and cause an even greater crisis of confidence in the clergy than that already apparent. It was probably as well, therefore, that mass public attention was upon other events.

A true and perfect

Relation

Of the Tryal and Condemnation, Execution and
last Speech of that unfortunate Gentleman

Mr. Robert Foulks

Late Minister of a Parish near *Ludlow* in *Shropshire*, who
Received Sentence of Death in *London*, for Murder and Adultery, and accordingly was carried privately in a Coach
to the place of Execution, on *Fryday* the last
of *January* 1678

Also his behaviour in Prison, both before and after Sentence, with his Speech to the People at the
place of Execution, and the words of his Text.
Published for to satisfy all people that are incensed with base and foolish Reports
on this unhappy man.

LIKEWISE

The Tryal, Condemnation and Execution of
two grand Traytors, *will. Ireland* and *John Grove*
both Jesuits, being the persons that was hired
to Kill his Majesty.

Let him that standeth take heed least he fall.

𝔚𝔦𝔱𝔥 𝔄𝔩𝔩𝔬𝔴𝔞𝔫𝔠𝔢.

Printed for *L. White* in *white-cross street.* 1679

166

A *Trew and perfect Relation of the Tryal and Condemnation, Execution and last Speech of that unfortunate Gentleman, Mr. Robert Foulks, late Minister &c.*

The Impious Actors, and Inhumane contrivers of the late Hellish plot, have in many circumstances shewn themselves so remarkably unworthy and extreamly disingenuous, that we cannot imagine but every Loyal Subject and good Christian will rejoyce to hear that the impartial hand of Over-ruling Justice hath brought any of them to their long deserved Punishment. And therefore we concluded that the Condemnation, Confession, and Execution, of those two grand Traytors William Ireland, and John Grove, whose crimes were no less than High Treason, and that too aggravated to the very heighth, could not but be welcome to all those true English hearts, who harbor any respect either for their King, Countrey or Religion; or indeed for themselves, their Estates, lives, wives, or Children; all these were subtly Level'd at in that Hellish contrivance, in which black Tragedy these, Grove and Ireland were to have Acted the most bloody part, for which they were brought to a fair Tryal at the Old Baily, where it was proved by good Evidence that they (with another) were to have kill'd the King, for which one of them was to have 1500 l. and the other thirty thousand Masses, (which he vallu'd at the same Rate) one of them presented a Pistol at him in St. James's Park, but the flint falling out, he was at that time disappointed. In fine they all three received Sentence of Death, and these two only (the other being suspended) were Drawn in a Sledge to the place of

Execution, where they still continued in the same obstinacy and stubbornness as they had done in Prison. Grove said nothing but a few Prayers in private, and so was turn'd off, but Ireland made in part a Confession, for he acknowledged, he had been a Jesuite a long time, and had done all he was able to convert as many as he could to the Popish Religion: this is the summ of what in more words he there delivered. After which both he and the other were hang'd up by the Neck, and cut down whilst some life remain in them, afterwards their breasts were ript open, their hearts taken out, their bodies quartered, and the same day buried in St. Giles in the Fields.

Before I enter on the other dismal and Tragical story, promised you in the Title, methinks I cannot but seriously contemplate How little and inconsiderable we are meerly of our selves, and how vainly we trust in our frail abilities! especially when by dayly experience I sadly observe, that the Great Almighty no sooner leaves us to the indirect motion of our natural courses, but as if we were in Love with our own Ruine, we presently run headlong into the black stream of Vice and Impiety, which is the only Current can conduct us to it; Our Reason which should be our Pilot, then serves us in no stead; no happy birth, Litterate Education, or sacred Function is able to bribe us to study our own good: but on the contrary, our predominant corruptions overruling them all, too often hurry us into those miserable premunires of Sin and Guilt, which we cannot get out of but with the vissible hazard both of Life and Soul.

This is the Truth we have sadly seen experienced by many, but particularly by this Mr. Rob. Foulks, of whom we are now about to discourse.

His living Relations, how neer soever they might be of Kin to him, could not possibly be related to his Crime, and therefore we shall let them quietly slumber in their old innocence, and only content ourselves to let the Reader understand that Mr. Foulks was late Minister of a place called Stanton Hay, not far from Ludlow in Shropshire, in which Benefice he Officiated when he was first challenged with this horrid Fact. The proceedings against him at the Sessions house in the Old Bayly in London were as followeth.

He and a young Gentlewoman, committed to his chargs, were both call'd to the Bar, and formally Indicted of Murther, to which they pleaded Not Guilty; but the Evidence against him was very clear and apparent, for it was prov'd that Mr. Foulks was left Guardian to the Gentlewoman Arraing'd with him, and making use of some Authority might be challenged from that trust, he with that, and urgent intreaties, gaind so far on her, as at last to debauch her to his bed, and had used that familiarity so often that at last she prov'd with Child, which not willing his neighbours should be acquainted with, he brought her (under pretence of preferring her) to London, and took lodgings for her in York Buildings in the Strand, resolving to stay with her till the pains of Delivery should be over, at length the fatal hour of her dreaded Travel approacht, and she by her lowd shrieks began to call for the welcome assistance of her own Sex, which is both decent and necessary in cases of that nature, but that it seems was utterly denied her by Mr. Foulks, who sternly oblig'd her to silence, protesting no body should perform that Office but himself.

What pangs the poor woman endured by so painful a Delivery is best judg'd by those who have been experienced in those labours; but the wicked intent of this barbarous usage, could referr to nothing but the designed destruction of the unfortunate babe, whom he no sooner receiv'd into the world, but he cruelly cram'd it down a house of Office; this was absolutely prov'd against him by several witnesses, nor was it deny'd by the miserable Gentlewoman, who was altogether ignorant of what he had done, till he himself had inform'd her what he had done with the murdered infant; the next morning when as he thought he had done his business very securely, he went down into Shropshire, but had not been long there, before the indisposition of the green woman, gave her attendant sufficient evidence she had been Delivered of a Child, which at last she confest; and it being thus positively prov'd against him, he was Condemned, and she not in the least consenting to the Murder, was both pittied and acquitted.

But however obstinate Mr. Foulks seem'd in his Tryal, he quickly chang'd his carriage after Condemnation, for then he not only openly acknowledged his Guilt, but very sorrowfully bewail'd the heynous nature of his horrid crime, which on better consideration he said, appeard to him in so terrible a shape, that it discompos'd and affrighted his very Soul.

Being return'd to Prison, he was often heard to say, That the apprehensions of death officiously attended with the terrible Ritinue of pain and ignomie, did not half so much affright him as the suddenness of it; that it was Judgement and not death that dejected him; however, he was not so discouraged but that he presently set himself about disposing his Soul into a fit posture to take her everlasting flight, which he concluded would have been with the other Offenders on the next Wednesday after the Friday on which he received Sentence, so short a time of preparation therefore made him so swift in it, that he would hardly afford himself time either to eat, drink or sleep, but thought every Minute ill spent wherein he did not exercise that Penitence, Sorrow, and contrition of spirit which was becomming so great an Offender, so that like holy David, he could truly say that Tears were his meat and drink day and night.

He was often heard to bemoan next to his guilt, that disgrace and ignomy his bad example might draw on the worthy Members of the Church; but he hoped that to the wise and Learned, his single failing would bring no scandal or reproach, on whose wholesome Principles which utterly forbid all such wild extravagancies: and that these hopes he more comfortably persisted in, as well because of his unfeigned sorrow, and Repentance for his horrid crime, as that the Doctrine Discipline, the Orders and Canons of the Church of England do in themselves appear to all men so exactly fit for the promotion and incouragement of Holiness Sobriety, Chastity, and all kind of Christian Virtues which contribute to a good Life; that she would be able to vindicate her self against all Scandals and Reproaches which might be thrown on her either by his or any other particular members misdemeanor.

By this decent behaviour, and exceeding others in Piety and Repentance, he became generally pittied by all that came near him, or heard of him; but among the rest, many Eminent Divines in London came to visit him, and being incouraged by those unusual signs of remorse and penitency which they beheld in him, they agreed on a private Fast to be kept in Newgate for him, which was accordingly performed, he joyning with them in a more fervent manner that ever was observ'd in any in his condition.

When the succeeding Wednesday, on which he thought he should have dy'd, was come, instead of the sad news of Execution, he had brought him a Reprieve, which suspended him for about Nine dayes longer, at which he was very much rejoyced, not that he had any hopes or desire to live, but that he might be more prepared to dy, and as if he had no other thoughts indeed, he grew still more earnest and laborious to make his Calling and Election sure than ever, imploying on himself long and voluntary Fasts, both from sleep and sustenance, that he might not lose any of that welcome time, indulgent Authority had so graciously afforded him.

And that he himself might proclaim his Repentance as lowd as the world had his crime, when he had spent great part of the day in Prayer and Ejaculations he imploy'd the other part of it and most of the night in writing down his Meditations, and what ever else he thought might be powerful to perswade all men, in time from committing his sins, lest when it is too late, they share with him in his guilt and sufferings, to which end he sent pious Letters to his Wife, Children and Parishoners, meerly for that purpose.

But still zealous that all himself could perform for the expiation of this publick, as well as other his private sins, he was careful to prepare an excellent Prayer fitted for his occasion, which he transcribed with his own hand, and caused to be sent to most Churches in London, on the 30th. of January, that being a Fast day strictly kept for the Murder of King Charles the First, so that by this means he was earnestly pray'd for, through the whole City; To conclude, there was nothing of Piety omitted by him which could possibly have been perfomed by or expected from him, either as he was a Christian, a Minister, or one so near his end.

To Conclude, When the fatal and appointed day of Execution came, he was brought out of the Press-Yard about ten of the Clock in the Morning, and in a Coach conveyed to Tyburn, accompanied thither with several Eminent Divines, who were mightily satisfied to see him cheerfully undergoe that great Work, with that constant Piety and Resolution which he had Exercised in Newgate. When he was got on the Ladder, he made a very excellent Speech to the People, to disswade them from those wicked courses which had brought him to that ignominious End. The perticulars cannot be expected here, but the sum of it was this.

My Friends and Brethren.

I am deservedly brought hither this day to suffer Death for a crime which deserves that Punishment by the Law, and I thank my great God I am too conscious of my own guilt in the least to deny but that both by the Laws of God and man, I have thereby forfeited that Life which I am now going to lay down; the horrid sin that I was sentenced for, was its true very great in itself, but yet is much aggrevated being done by one of my Function or Calling, and it is one of the greatest fears I have now left me in the world, least my Example should contract any contempt on the Renowned Clergy-men of England. Ah Sirs, it was not the Church, but one of her unworthy members that committed this heynous offence; and therefore whatsoever you think me, for God sake let her remain pure and unblemisht, as indeed she is, in your hearts and minds: Had I followed the wholesome Principles she enjoys, both me and all men too, I had not been in this place upon this occasion: but here are several Learned and pious Ministers that can in part manifest my cordial and unfeigned sorrow, for having thus shamefully offended both God and her; and I hope the great God, whose face I trust I shall in a few minutes behold, doth both see my contrition, and will through the benefits of the blood of Jesus accept me for it, O therefore I beseech you, if my ill Example has disrepresented her, let my last Penitence and dying hatred and abhorrency of so black a sin recommend her again to your practice and obedience, without which you must never expect to be happy.

His Speech was much longer, but the greatness of the crowd hindred us from hearing all, but the substance we have here Related. After he had thus done he pray'd very earnestly, and then freely submitted to the Execution of the Sentence.

His Corps were privately brought back in a Coach that Evening and decently buried at St. Giles in the Fields.

POSTSCRIPT

Thus ended this unfortunate Gentleman, who by temptations of Satan was thus brought like Holy David into the horrid sin of Adultery but as his sin resembled his so did his Repentance, and we hope they are both now singing Hallelujahs in the glorious Region of Eternal joy.

FINIS

THE

EXECUTION

OF

Mr Rob. Foulks

Late Minifter of *Stanton-Lacy*

IN

SHROPSHIRE.

MR. ROBERT FOULKS received sentence of Death at the last Sessions, for killing a new-born Child in November last in York-buildings in the Strand, from whence the same morning he went out of Town; but after the discovery of the murdered Infant, being pursued, was apprehended in the Country, and brought up to Tryal as aforesaid: The fact was too apparent, nor did he after conviction offer to deny it, but rather made it his business to give Glory to God by an open confession of his sins, and declaration of his sorrow and self-abhorrency for them. That he might the more effectually accomplish this, Authority was graciously pleased to allow him some longer time, than commonly is graunted, to fit himself for death.

These few days so charitably indulg'd, he fail'd not to improve, but husbanded them with diligence to the best advantage; confession of his sins with all their aggravations, bewailing them with bitter tears, and begging forgiveness, as well for the guilt as scandal of them, was his continual imployment. He was visited by several of the most Eminent, Learned and Godly Divines about the City, who, at diverse times, came to give him their advice, and afford him the comfort of their Christian Offices and Prayers, which he receiv'd with all thankfulness; so that they departed much satisfied.

Let not therefore, either the right or left-hand Enemies triumph, or cast reflections and reproaches on this occasion; ··· Crimine ab uno disce omnes ··· is but Poetical Logick, The charity of Divinity will never allow any brand or stigmatize a whole party for the lapses of any single Member, when the Body gives no connivance or approbation to such excesses: The Doctrine and Discipline, the Orders and Canons of the Church of England, every way fitted for encouragement of holiness of life, sobriety, chastity, and all kind of Christian vertues and practical piety, are sufficient to justifie her to all the considerate World, against such ignominious scandals and undeserved obloquies: And as her Principles are the soundest and purest, so through Gods Grace, she is furnisht with as Learned and Godly a Clergy in general, as any Nation under Heaven; able, both by their Doctrine, and by their exemplary lives and conversations, to put to silence such malicious cavillers. As this poor Gentleman, led away by the temptations of Satan and his own evil nature, for want of keeping a due watch over his heart, and turning away his eyes from vanity, came to fall like David, into those blackest of sins, Adultery and Murder; so we have good grounds, from his later behaviour, in the judgment of chastity, to hope, and believe, that he has imitated that Royal Penitent too, in contrition and hearty sorrow for those crying crimes, and that by the grace of God, and merits of our blessed Lord and Saviour Jesus Christ, he may be washed and purged from those, and all other pollutions, and cloathed with the Robes of the Lambs Righteousness; may be admitted into the blissful Regions of everlasting Glory, where nothing impure may enter.

As for the particulars of his deportment, penitent Carriage, and Religious Conversation, since the time of his Condemnation, to that of his Dissolution, all that visited him (amongst whom were many Worthy Divines as aforesaid) can bear Testimony: and farther, that he might glorifie God in his death, whom he had dishonoured so much in his Life, endeavouring if possible to make his Repentance, and acknowledgment of his Sins, as publique as the scandal of them had been. He imployd the few moments he had to live, in Writing down his Meditations, and giving a warning to Sinners, by his sad, but remarkable Example; and directing several Letters to his Wife, Children, Parishoners and other friends, which being all Compleated under his own hand, and delivered to very Worthy and Reverend Persons, are to be made publick: A work which (with the Divine blessing) may prove of great use and advantage to Souls.

Some few days before that of his Execution, he humbly received the Sacrament of the Lords Supper, and kept several private Fasts. The day before he suffered (being the Anniversary Fast, and Humiliation for the horrid Murther of King Charles the First, of blessed Memory) he was at his own request Solemnly prayed for, in most of the Churches of London and Westminster, and expressed great rejoycing in his Spirit, that his days were lengthened out so long in the Land of the Living, contrary to his Expectation, that he might have the opportunity of enjoying the publick Prayers of so many good Christians.

On Friday the 31st. of Jan. 1678/9. about ten of the Clock in the forenoon, he was brought out of the Press-yard, and in a Coach conveyed to the place of Execution, where he made an Excellent Confession and Speech to the People. A Copy of which having it ready Written, (with his own hand) he there delivered to a Minister present, to be faithfully Printed with the rest of his Papers which are now in the Press, and within very few days will be made publick.

And so having prayed very affectionately, freely submitted himself to the Execution of the Sentence.

His Corpse were brought back in a Coach, and that Evening decently (but privately) Interr'd at St. Gileses.

FINIS

Will of Elizabeth Atkinson
dated 10th March 1681/82

Herefordshire Record Office: at ref. AA20 106/2/18

In the name of God Amen the tenth day of March Anno Regni Regi Caroli secundi nunc Angliae &c xxxiiijo Annoque Domini 1681o I Elizabeth Attkinson of Stanton Lacy in the County of Salop widow being sick in body but of Sound and perfect memory disposing sence & understanding and having a Serious Intention & resolution to settle and dispose of my Estate doe make and declare this my last will and Testament in manner & forme following (Vizt) **Inprimis** I Commend my Soule into the hands of Almighty God that gave it and my body to the earth from whence it was taken to be decently buryed in the parish Church of Stanton Lacy aforesaid and as neare as may be to my Deare husband Thomas Attkinson Clerke, deceased **Item** I give and bequeath to my Daughter in law Anne Attkinson my Silver Cawdle Cup and one Silver porringer with all the Furniture in a Chamber called the yellow chamber in the house wherein I now dwell **Item** I give & bequeath unto my Sonn in Law Francis Attkinson Clerke and his wife twenty Shillings a peece to buy them rings **Item** I give and bequeath unto my Sister Maud Tracy fourty Shillings to buy her a ring (If she be living) **Item** I give and bequeath unto my Neece Mary Hopton five pounds to be payd her within six months after my decease by my Executor herein after named **Item** I give & bequeath unto my Neece Elizabeth Cole widow twenty Shillings to buy her a ring **Item** I give devise and bequeath All and singular the rest and residue of my goodes Cattles Chattles Creditts Bookes

Plate and personall Estate whatsoever unto my Sonn in Law
John Attkinson Gent. he defraying my Debts and Funerall
Expenses And I doe nominate & appoinct my Sayd Son in Law
John Attkinson Sole Executor of this my last will & Testament
Revoking all & every will and Testament by me att any time
formerly made In Wittness whereof I have hereunto put my
hand & Seale the day & yeare first above written

Signed Sealed and published
In the presence of us

Elizabeth Attkinson

Rich. Hopley Junr
    Signum
Annae A Hanson
    Hen. Bishop

Sworn and proved at Ludlow before Sir Timothy Baldwyn
18th February 1689/90

[Buried 27th June 1689 at Stanton Lacy]

DOCUMENT 10

Letter from the Bishop of St Asaph, William Lloyd, to Archbishop of Canterbury William Sancroft

Dated 3rd January 1682/83
(extract from a longer letter about several matters)

Bodleian Library, Oxford: MS Tanner 35, folios 159r & 159v

May it please your Grace

...There is another thing which I think myself obliged to acquaint your Grace with because it has happen'd in my Neighborhood, & I think it is not fit that such things should be kept from your Graces knowledge. There was one Fowks Rector of Stanton Lacy neer Ludlow that was hang'd at Tiburn neer 3 yeers ago for the murder of a bastard that he had by one Anne Atkinson in the parish of St. Martin-in-the-fields. I was often with him before his death, & once or twice with his Concubin in her lying in, & from them both I assuredly know that she was as guilty as he of the murder. She had one bastard by him before that is living. She had procur'd severall Abortions, & had used all the means she could think of to destroy this very Child in her body. Which notwithstanding all those attempts being born when onely they 2 were in a chamber together, he receiv'd it into the world & askt what he should do with it, She bad him kill it & gave him the knife with which he kill'd it, & when he had thrown it into the house of office she went half an hour after with a curtain rod with which she thrust it down out of sight. After all this, the body being found by Gods wonderfull Providence, they were both of them arraigned at

181

the old Baily where, tho' her being deliver'd without a Midwife was evidence enough against her, yet having great friends she was acquitted by Justice Scrogs, & Fowks was convict by no other but her single Testimony. I was with him that night which was the first time I ever saw him & then was she as Jolly as he was sad, enterteining her Lawyers at the Tavern & has continued ever since, insensible of the Judgements of God. This horrible woman stood at that time presented at Hereford in the Ecclesiastical Court for suspicion of Incontinence, which was all that the Churchwardens could charge her with. But when she was gone to London there was no farther proceeding against her. Ever since she has kept out of the Countrey till this Summer when, having made friends in the Ecclesiasticall Court, she made bold to appear & there being nothing proved against her she was dismist without any Censure. Sir Timothy Baldwin who is Judge of that Court knew all her story, & had promis'd Fowks'es widow that he would make the wicked woman do penance in every Church in the diocese or pay such a com[m]utation as should maintein her & her 4 Children. But he was content not to be present at this Justice, & his Surveyor that acted for him confest he was asham'd of it. The morning before he dismist her, but he said he must dismiss her for he had order to do it. All good men are amaz'd at this, the Churches enemies triumph, & the Countrey hold their noses at our disciplin. But it is onely Hereford disciplin, & I hope your Grace will finde some handle to take hold of it & then I doubt not you will so order them for this peece of Justice that it shall stink no farther than to that Church.

Jan 3. 1682 [/83]
W Asaph

DOCUMENT 11

Letter from the Bishop of St Asaph, William Lloyd, to Archbishop of Canterbury William Sancroft

Dated 31st January 1682/83
(extract from a longer letter about several matters)

Bodleian Library, Oxford: MS Tanner 35, folio 171r

My Good Lord

Your Grace had been pleased to draw Trouble upon yourself by sending me the register of Hereford's Letter. For I see that those who have little sens of Conscience or shame have yet some regard to your Grace's displeasure, & will do that for fear of it which they would not have done otherwise, for the discharge of their duty or to avoid the clamor of the Countrey. I do not at all doubt my Information, that that most flagitious woman has both Summer'd & winter'd at Stanton, the place where she had her bastard that is now living & where she was presented for that which was murther'd, is most tru. And there she might have remained a living moniment of the shame of that Court. For that she was discharged openly in the Court, I was told by Mrs Fowks, who said she had it from the surrogates mouth the same day when he excus'd himself to her for doing it. But now your Grace has been pleas'd to take notice of it, I doubt not somthing will be done for the removing of this horrible Scandall.

> My Lord Your Graces most obliged
> & most obedient son & servant
> Jan. 31. 82 [/83]   W. Asaph

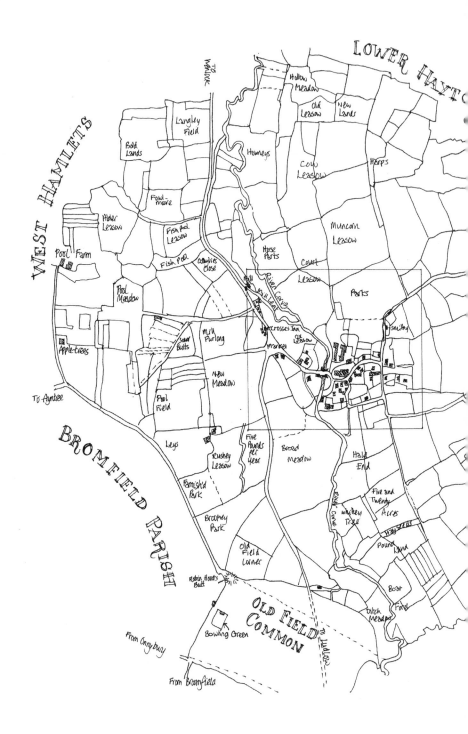

A
MAP
of part of the
MANOR
of
STANTON
Lacey
1770

The village of Stanton Lacy lies at the south-western corner of the northern portion of the parish, close to its boundary with Bromfield. This map is based on one of 1770, the earliest to survive, showing the village very much as Foulkes would have known it. Compared with today, there are many more buildings, particularly between the river bridge and the triangular medieval market, an area today occupied by fields. The market, at the junction of three roads, is today much reduced in size, and at its northern corner was the Crosses Inn, probably that occupied by William Hopton. To the south of Robin Hood's Butt was widow Partridge's bowling green on Old Field, clearly marked on a map of 1733, and still there in 1847.

The Atkinson family tree

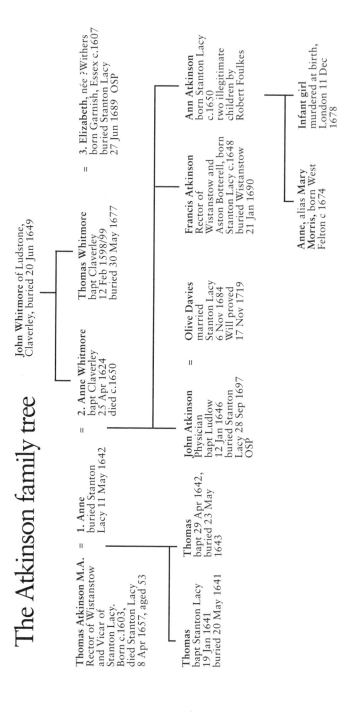

John Whitmore of Ludstone, Claverley, buried 20 Jun 1649

Thomas Atkinson M.A. = 1. Anne buried Stanton Lacy 11 May 1642
Rector of Wistanstow and Vicar of Stanton Lacy.
Born c.1603, died Stanton Lacy 8 Apr 1657, aged 53

= 2. Anne Whitmore bapt Claverley 25 Apr 1624 died c.1650

Thomas Whitmore bapt Claverley 12 Feb 1598/99 buried 30 May 1677

= 3. Elizabeth, née ?Withers born Garnish, Essex c.1607 buried Stanton Lacy 27 Jun 1689 OSP

Thomas
bapt Stanton Lacy 19 Jan 1641 buried 20 May 1641

Thomas
bapt 29 Apr 1642, buried 23 May 1643

John Atkinson
Physician bapt Ludlow 12 Jan 1646 buried Stanton Lacy 28 Sep 1697 OSP

= Olive Davies married Stanton Lacy 6 Nov 1684 Will proved 17 Nov 1719

Francis Atkinson
Rector of Wistanstow and Aston Botterell, born Stanton Lacy c.1648 buried Wistanstow 21 Jan 1690

Ann Atkinson
born Stanton Lacy c.1650 two illegitimate children by Robert Foulkes

Anne, alias Mary Morris, born West Felton c 1674

Infant girl
murdered at birth, London 11 Dec 1678

186

The Whitmore / Craven family tree

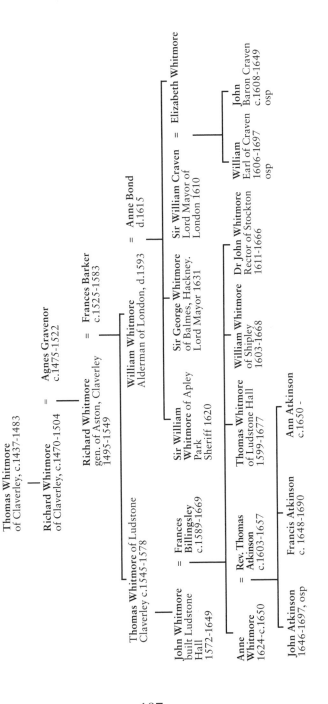

Thomas Whitmore
of Claverley, c.1437-1483

Richard Whitmore = Agnes Gravenor
of Claverley, c.1470-1504   c.1475-1522

Richard Whitmore = Frances Barker
gen. of Aston, Claverley   c.1525-1583
1495-1549

William Whitmore = Anne Bond
Alderman of London, d.1593   d.1615

Thomas Whitmore of Ludstone
Claverley c.1545-1578

Sir William
Whitmore of Apley
Park
Sheriff 1620

Sir George Whitmore
of Balmes, Hackney.
Lord Mayor 1631

Sir William Craven
Lord Mayor of
London 1610

Elizabeth Whitmore

John Whitmore = Frances
built Ludstone   Billingsley
Hall   c.1589-1669
1572-1649

Thomas Whitmore
of Ludstone Hall
1599-1677

William Whitmore
of Shipley
1603-1668

Dr John Whitmore
Rector of Stockton
1611-1666

William
Earl of Craven
1606-1697
osp

John
Baron Craven
c.1608-1649
osp

Anne = Rev. Thomas
Whitmore   Atkinson
1624-c.1650   c.1603-1657

Ann Atkinson
c.1650 -

Francis Atkinson
c. 1648-1690

John Atkinson
1646-1697, osp

Select Bibliography

MANUSCRIPT SOURCES

Bodleian Library, *MS. Tanner 35*, ff. 159r, 159v, 171r;
  MS. Tanner 147, ff. 184-5, 232

Bodleian Library, *MS. J Walker* c. 3, fo. 206

Herefordshire Record Office:
  Foulkes Case Papers & Depositions, boxed at HD4/25 & HD4/26

  Ludlow Archdeaconry Court Book (Acts of Instance) 1673-1677, HD4/1/66

  Ludlow Archdeaconry Deposition Book, (Office promoted by Ralph, Lord Eure, contra Daniel Cage), HD4/2/16A

  Ludlow Archdeaconry Deposition Book 1674-76, HD4/2/16B

  Ludlow Deanery Court Book (Acts of Office), *1673-1680*, HD4/1/235

  Registrars Files, HD7/20/355

  Will of Elizabeth Atkinson, 1682, AA20 106/2/18

  Will of Francis Atkinson, 1690, AA20 106/2/20

London Metropolitan Archives: *Gaol Delivery Roll for the Middlesex Sessions*, ref. MJ/SR/1556

National Library of Wales, *Parish Register Mallwyd No 1*

National Library of Wales, *Powis Papers*, 14226

The National Archives: *Will of Thomas Atkinson, 1657*, Prob. 11/273, fo.188v

The National Archives: *Will of Thomas Whitmore, 1676*, Prob. 11/354, fo.198r

The National Archives: *Will of William Whitmore, 1667*, Prob. 11/328 fo.288v

Shropshire Archives, MS 320/6; *Estate Book of Thomas Powys 1665-1670*

Worcestershire Record Office, *Liber Recordum for 1666-7*, ref. A1. box 9

CONTEMPORARY PRINTED SOURCES

Dunton, J., *Athenian Gazette, or Casuistical Mercury*, Volume 4, No.16.

Dunton, J., *The Wonders of Free-Grace: Or, A Compleat History Of all the Remarkable Penitents that have been Executed at Tyburn, and elsewhere for these last Thirty Years*, London, Printed for John Dunton at the Raven in the Poultry, 1690

The Execution of Mr. Rob. Foulks, late Minister of Stanton-Lacy in Shropshire, London: Printed for R.G. 1679

Foulkes, R., *An Alarme for Sinners*, London, Printed for Langley Curtis, on Ludgate-Hill, 1679

The Shropshire Amazement, (London, 1708) [Bodleian Library, Vet. A3 e.237 (50)]

A true and perfect Relation of the Tryal and Condemnation, Execution and last Speech of that unfortunate Gentleman Mr. Robert Foulks, London: Printed for L. White in White-cross street, 1679

LATER PRINTED SOURCES

Auden, J.E. ed., *Shrewsbury School Register, 1636-1664*, (Shrewsbury 1917)

Calendar of the County Committee for Compounding; Cases (1643-1660)

Calendar of State Papers, Domestic Series: Charles I (1637)

Chapman, C.R., *Ecclesiastical Courts, Officials & Records*, (Dursley, 1997)

Clark, A., *The Life and Times of Anthony à Wood*, ii (Oxford, 1892)

Daily Mail, 2 Dec 1968

Dictionary of National Biography (1938)

Faraday, M.A., 'The Ludlow Poll-Tax Returns of 1667', in *Transactions of the Shropshire Archaeological Society*, **LIX** (1971/72)

Foster, J., *Alumni Oxonienses 1500-1714*

Goldie, M. ed., *The Entring Book of Roger Morrice*, ii (London, 2007)

Hearth Tax Collectors Book for Worcester 1678-1680,
Worcestershire Historical Society, n.s. **11**

Ingram, M., *Church Courts, Sex and Marriage in England, 1570-1640*, Cambridge 1987 (1990 edition)

Kenyon, J., *The Popish Plot* (London 1972, repr. 2000)

Lewis, S., *Topographical Dictionary of Wales*, ii (3rd edit. 1845)

Lloyd, L.C., *The Inns of Shrewsbury* (Shrewsbury, 1942)

Matthews, A.G., *Walker Revised* (Oxford, 1948; repr. 1988)

Moir, A.L., *Bromfield Priory and Church* (Chester, 1947)

Montgomeryshire Collections, **IX** (1876)

Montgomeryshire Collections, **69** (1981)

Oxford Dictionary of National Biography (2004)

Picard L., *Restoration London* (London, 1997)

Privy Council Register v (Jan–Apr 1638/39), HMSO 1968

Rayner, J.L., & Crook, G.T., (eds.), *The Complete Newgate Calendar*, i (Navarre Society, London, 1926)

Ripley, P., 'A Seventeenth-Century Consistory Court Case' in *Bristol and Gloucestershire Archaeological Society Transactions*, C (1982)

Rimmer A. & Adnitt H.W., *History of Shrewsbury School* (Shrewsbury, 1889)

Sharpe, J.A., *Early Modern England* (2nd edit., 1997)

Spaeth, D.A., *The Church in an Age of Danger: Parsons and Parishioners 1660-1740* (Cambridge, 2000)

Spaeth, D.A., 'Common Prayer? Popular observance of the Anglican liturgy in Restoration Wiltshire', in Susan Wright (ed.), *Parish Church & People; Local Studies in Lay Religion 1350-1750* (London, 1988)

Shropshire Parish Registers (Hereford Diocese v – Bromfield)

Shropshire Parish Registers (Hereford Diocese x – Claverley)

Shropshire Parish Registers (Hereford Diocese xiii, xiv – Ludlow)

Shropshire Parish Registers (Hereford Diocese xviii – Onibury)

Shropshire Parish Registers (Hereford Diocese iv – Stanton Lacy)

Shropshire Star, 29 Nov 1968

Stackhouse Acton, Mrs. F., *Castles & Old Mansions of Shropshire*, (Shrewsbury, 1868)

Transactions of the Shropshire Archaeological Society, 4th ser. **II**

Victoria County History of Shropshire, **II** (Oxford, 1973)

Walker J., *An Attempt towards Recovering an Account of the Numbers and Sufferings of the Clergy of the Church of England etc.* (London, 1714)

Waller, M., *1700 Scenes from London Life,* (London, 2000),

Watkins-Pitchford, W., *The Shropshire Hearth-Tax Roll of 1672*, (Shropshire Archaeological Society, Shrewsbury, 1949)

Watts, S. ed., *Glebe Terriers of Shropshire*, Part 2 (Shropshire Record Series 6, 2002),

Whitelocke, B., *Memorials of the English Affairs* (London, 1732)

Whiteman, A. ed., *The Compton Census of 1676: A Critical Edition* (British Academy Records of Social & Economic History, n.s. **X**, 1986)

Wilson, J.B. ed., *The Parish Book of St. Helen's Church in Worcester,* i (London, 1900)

Wood, Anthony à, *Athenae Oxonienses* (Bliss ed., 1817), **iii**

Wright, T, *Ludlow Sketches* (Ludlow, 1867)

Footnotes

Abbreviations:
DNB Dictionary of National Biography; **HRO** Herefordshire Record Office; **ODNB Oxford Dictionary of National Biography 2004; SA** Shropshire Archives; **TNA** The National Archives

1. *Shropshire Star*, 29 Nov 1968; *Daily Mail*, 2 Dec 1968

2. Before the adoption of the Gregorian calendar in 1752, the civil and legal New Years Day was upon Lady Day, the 25th of March. The last day of the old year was therefore March 24th. What we would today call the 31st January 1679 was then regarded as being in 1678. To avoid confusion, even at that time, it was often referred to as the 31st January 1678/79

3. The Compton Census returned a rounded population figure of 400, but this excluded children under the age of sixteen. See: ed. A Whiteman, *The Compton Census of 1676: A Critical Edition* (British Academy Records of Social & Economic History, n.s. X, 1986), 255

4. HRO: AA/20, box 21, no. 89

5. *Calendar of State Papers Domestic: Charles I* (1637), 279/280

6. *Ibid.* (1637/38), 505

7. *Ibid.* (1638/39), 339

8. *Privy Council Register* (Jan–Apr 1638/39), HMSO 1968, 22, 37

9. *Calendar of the County Committee for Compounding; Cases (1643-1660)*, 2838; dated 24th June 1651. On 16th March 1651 the Parliamentary commissioners seized and sequestered all Lord Craven's estates and property, and an Act for their sale was passed in August 1652

10. *Lingua acrioris iudicii limatior interpres*

11. See *Shropshire Parish Registers (Hereford Diocese iv – Stanton Lacy)*, 1, 2 & passim. The 'impropriation' of the rectory of Stanton Lacy harks back to its early history, when it was given to the Augustinian priory of Llanthony Prima by Hugh de Lacy shortly after 1103. At the priory's dissolution in 1536, the rights to take the rectoral or great tithe and to nominate a vicar were acquired from the Crown by an 'impropriator', an individual who held them as his own private property. By 1639 this was the lord of the manor, John Craven; but by the time of the Commonwealth either he or his elder brother and

successor, William Lord Craven, had leased the right to gather the rectoral tithe to a separate lessee for each township

12. This is mentioned in Thomas Atkinson's will, made 6th April 1657. The National Archives (hereinafter TNA) Prob. 11/273, fo. 188v

13. Bodleian Library, MS J Walker c 3, fo. 206. Walker questioned whether the Thomas Atkinson of Wistanstow and Stanton Lacy was one and the same man, but there is no doubt of this. The fact that Atkinson's son Francis later succeeded as rector at Wistanstow may have confused him

14. TNA: Prob. 11/273, fo. 188v (see Appendix, document 1)

15. J Walker, *An Attempt towards Recovering an Account of the Numbers and Sufferings of the Clergy of the Church of England etc.* (London, 1714), 185 A.G. Matthews, Walker Revised (Oxford 1948, repr. 1988), 303. A Major Slaughter had held out at Cardigan Castle, for a fortnight in December 1644, on behalf of the royalist Colonel Gerard, before being captured after its walls were breached by a Parliamentary relieving force. If this is the man, he sounds far from an obvious candidate as a parish minister under the Commonwealth. B. Whitelocke, *Memorials of the English Affairs* (London 1732), 130

16. *Stanton Lacy Parish Register*, 56-9

17. *Ludlow Parish Register*, 403. Anne Whitmore of Ludstone Hall was baptized in Claverley parish church on the 25th April 1624. She was also second cousin to the two Lord Cravens, whose mother had been Elizabeth Whitmore of London

18. Ann's mother's second eldest brother, William, born in 1603, was named as the children's uncle and guardian in Thomas Atkinson's will, and appears to have been close to him. William Whitmore, of Shipley in Claverley parish, died in June 1668, six months after making his last will (see page 145, and also note 102)

19. DNB (1938), vii, 515; *Oxford Dictionary of National Biography* (2004), x, 552-3

20. HRO: *Ludlow Archdeaconry Deposition Book 1667-1674*, HD4/2/16A, fo. 188v

21. National Library of Wales, *Parish Register Mallwyd No 1*. Both baptisms were probably performed by Dr. John Davies, rector of Mallwyd from 1604 until his death in 1644. One of the most eminent scholars of his time, Davies helped to prepare the Welsh edition of the bible published in 1620, and in 1632 compiled the first Welsh-Latin

dictionary. He was cheerful, kind, and benevolent, and after disastrous floods in 1633 he replaced three local bridges at his own expence. In 1640 he rebuilt the chancel and bell-tower of his parish church; and by the mid 19th-century Mallwyd church was still 'remarkable for the situation of the altar in the centre, opposite the reading-desk, to which it was removed from the east end by Dr. Davies... in defiance of the injunction of Laud, Archbishop of Canterbury'. *Montgomeryshire Collections*, IX (1876), 369-373; ibid. 69 (1981), 83-88; S Lewis, *Topographical Dictionary of Wales*, ii, (3rd edit. 1845), 190

22. ed. J E Auden, *Shrewsbury School Register 1636-1664*, Shrewsbury 1917, 37

23. J Foster, *Alumni Oxonienses 1500-1714*, 522

24. Anthony à Wood, *Athenae Oxonienses* (Bliss ed., 1817), iii, 1195. A servitor was an undergraduate from a less well-to-do background who was assisted from college funds and given facilities to study, in return for doing menial tasks and waiting upon the more wealthy students in Hall

25. R Foulkes, *An Alarme for Sinners* (London, 1679), 4. The ordinations were performed in conjunction with Dr. Ralph Bathurst, who examined the candidates and acted as archdeacon. These usually took place in Skinner's parish of Launton, near Bicester, although occasionally also in the chapel of Trinity College. See DNB (1938), i, 1330; & ibid. xviii, 348

26. *Stanton Lacy Parish Register*, 67. Foulkes also recorded his marriage in the Stanton Lacy parish register, the Ludlow register having been suspended at the time. The wedding took place only five months after Thomas Atkinson's death, but Foulkes was adamant that he had never met him

27. *Transactions of the Shropshire Archaeological Society*, 4th ser. II, 212

28. Herefordshire Record Office: *Ludlow Deanery Court Book (Acts of Office)*, 1673-1680, at HD4/1/235, hereafter cited as '*Court Book*'; *Ludlow Archdeaconry Court Book (Acts of Instance) 1673-1677*, at HD4/1/66; *Ludlow Archdeaconry Deposition Book 1674-76*, at HD4/2/16B; and the Foulkes case papers & depositions boxed at HD4/25 & HD4/26

29. This was known as such simply because 'one Francis Hamonds and his sonne', John, were former tenants before the Atkinson family

arrived there (HD4/25, Foulkes v. Chearme, deposition by Edward Coats, 18th March 1678). It was the second largest house in the village, with seven hearths in 1672 (*The Shropshire Hearth-Tax Roll of 1672*, Shrewsbury 1949, 167). The identity of Hammonds Farm is at present unknown, the name probably long disused by the time of the Craven Estates Manorial Survey of 1770 (SA, at ref. 6001/2480)

30. Extract from deposition by Elizabeth Atkinson, taken 18th September 1677. From hereon, depositions will be cited simply by name and the date of examination, or, if not known, the date of 'exhibition' in court, i.e. HD4/26, E Atkinson, 18 Sept 1677

31. The vicarage in John Whateley's time is described in the 1607 Glebe Terrier as a house of six bays, with a single-bay cowhouse, stable, four-bay barn, and a garden and orchard of a quarter of an acre. It may be to this that Foulkes returned after 1662. Ten years later he was paying tax on five hearths. See ed S Watts, *Glebe Terriers of Shropshire, Part 2* (Shropshire Record Series 6, 2002), 114; *The Shropshire Hearth-Tax Roll of 1672*, (Shrewsbury 1949), 167

32. HD4/26, J Atkinson, 17 Sept 1677

33. HD4/26, Office contra Ann Atkinson, 1 Oct 1678

34. *Stanton Lacy Parish Register*, 83-4

35. Ibid.; and HD4/26, E Atkinson, 18 Sept 1677. Tithes from the several townships were taken by a group of lessees, one of whom was Elizabeth Atkinson. All of them were subsequently presented by bishop Croft in the consistory court during 1675 (for which see HD4/1/235, 22 June 1675). See also note 11

36. *An Alarme for Sinners*, 5

37. Will at HRO: 37/3/7, dated 30 Aug 1670, proved 8 Aug 1673

38. Seven witness statements in support of this court case are in the Deposition Book, *Office promoted by Ralph, Lord Eure, contra Daniel Cage*, at HD4/2/16A, fo.188r – 190v, 192r. Daniel Cage was also the father of Martha Dovey, born at Lindsey in Suffolk in 1632, who herself was to become embroiled in the Foulkes litigation. Like her aunt, she too had been married in Stanton Lacy parish church

39. J L Rayner & G T Crook (eds.), *The Complete Newgate Calendar*, i (Navarre Society, London, 1926), 274

40. *Ibid.*, 275. It reads: 'Foulkes ... took an opportunity of discovering a criminal passion for her, though he had at that time a virtuous wife and two children living'.

41. A brief entry occurs in the Consistory Court Book in October 1674 presenting Foulkes, but it is dismissed with no other comment (*Court Book*, fo. 22v). Richard Hopton senior was certainly making allegations at around this time, which he later denied when challenged; and Richard junior overheard Foulkes being accused to his face by an Elias Greaves (HD4/2/16B, R Hopton, 9 Oct 1676)

42. These were said to include an aunt at 'West Barnet', almost certainly Chipping Barnet, also an anonymous 'kinsman' in London. In 1674 she was accompanied to Worcester by 'a maid servant of the Lady Cravens'

43. HD4/26, G Coston, 3 Sept 1677

44. HD4/26, R Foulkes, 4 Sept 1677; HD4/2/16B, W Hopton, 28 Oct 1676; *Stanton Lacy Parish Register*, 54-5, 84. This money was originally raised by subscription in 1633, during John Whateley's incumbency, and Thomas Atkinson had added five pounds to it under the terms of his will in 1657

45. HD4/26, R Foulkes, 26 Feb 1678

46. Elizabeth said she was born at 'Garnish', in Essex, in about 1607. A Garnish Hall stands at Theydon Garnon, near Epping Forest. The parish church is close by, and a Dr. Henry Withers was rector there between 1591 and his death in 1609. The house is situated immediately south-east of what is today the M11/M25 interchange

47. HD4/26, R Foulkes, 26 Feb 1678

48. HD4/26, J Atkinson, 17 Sept 1677

49. HD4/2/16B, M Hopton, 28 Oct 1676. Another witness, Richard Chearme, said that Ann had then returned to Stanton Lacy for about seven weeks before going on elsewhere (HD4/2/16B, R Chearme, 30 Oct 1676). This evidence is seemingly contradicted by that of an Andrew Walker who testified that his brother, Edward, told him that he had taken Ann to Shrewsbury from West Felton, and 'from thence she took coach for London', at a time when it was rumoured that Foulkes had taken her from West Felton to Worcester (HD4/26, A Walker, 3 Sept 1677). One explanation is that there may have been more than one visit to West Felton. On the other hand these could be fragments of

a consistent story, and that it was intended that Ann should go direct to London, but that it was found that she was too weak to stand a gruelling ordeal over rough roads, and so had to break her journey to recuperate at home before travelling on

50. A recipe for such an ointment was published in *W M's The Queen's Closet Open'd* (London, 1696). See M Waller, *1700 Scenes from London Life*, (London, 2000), 55-6, 356

51. HD4/2/16B, R Hopton jnr., 9 Oct 1676; M Dovey, 28 Oct 1676

52. HD4/26, J Garbett, 5 Sept 1677 Lloyd had secured the lease of the castle in 1673. See P Brown, P King and P Remfry, 'Whittington Castle: the Marcher Fortress of the Fitz Warin Family' in *Transactions of the Shropshire Archaeological Society* LXXIX (2004), 120, citing NLW Aston Hall Deeds, 1264 (of 10 April 1673)

53. HD4/26, W Bradley, 5 Sept 1677

54. HD4/26, *Office contra Ann Atkinson*, 23 Jul 1678; R Hopton snr. & C Pearce, 20 Aug 1678. Another account (HD4/26, Ralph Fenton, 1 Sept 1677) suggested that the child might have been sent to nurse 'near Bridgnorth' for a time. Sending the child over the Welsh border, or to the Royal Peculiar of Bridgnorth, conveniently placed the baby outside the jurisdiction of the bishop of Hereford

55. HD4/26, C Pearce, 20 Aug 1678; & S Wall, 26 Feb 1678

56. HD4/2/16B, R Chearm, 30 Oct 1676; HD4/26, R Bowland, 18 Mar 1678

57. HD4/2/16B, M Dovey, 28 Oct 1676

58. HD4/26, J Slade, 26 Feb 1677; HD4/2/16B, W Hopton, 28 Oct 1676; R Chearme, 30 Oct 1676

59. HD4/2/16B, R Chearme, 30 Oct 1676

60. HD4/26. Exhibited 1 Aug 1676

61. *Court Book*, fo. 75v. This was, in fact, a stock formula, the wording later being adopted by the reforming movement in the reign of William III, following the Glorious Revolution of 1688

62. Martha Dovey was formerly Martha Cage, daughter of Daniel Cage (see note 38)

63. HD4/26, R Foulkes, 4 Sept 1677

64. HD4/26, E Smalman, attorney, 24 Sept 1677. Lord Eure's action was nominally against Daniel Cage, contesting the will of Lady Martha

Eure. Martha Hawkes, Daniel Cage's daughter, had been bequeathed but a modest ten pounds, worth about a thousand pounds today. Lord Eure could well have afforded to ignore it, but it seems to have become a matter of principle to him

65. In law, a marriage merely by 'declaration' was then perfectly legal, without any reference to their Church, in which the parties could sign documents to the effect that they now took each other as man and wife. However, such marriages, not being conducted 'in the sight of God', nor in the face of their local parish congregation, could always be open to question within a conservative parish community, as also liable to attack from the clergy. Hence few seem to have opted for it, but for the poor it was a cheap form of marriage, there being no fees, and it was also suitable for Quakers who would not take oaths

66. HD4/26, L Milner, 26 Sept 1677. Its full title is *The Royal Peculiar and Exempt Jurisdiction of Bridgnorth*, and its territory included the parishes of St Mary Magdalene and St Leonard's, Bridgnorth, Alverley, Claverley, and Quatford. Its autonomy placed it outside the jurisdiction of the bishop, and will have attracted those who wished to be married quickly in secret outside their own parishes. For a useful review of the issues surrounding marriages by licence, and also clandestine marriages, see D A Spaeth, *The Church in an Age of Danger: Parsons and Parishioners 1660-1740* (Cambridge, 2000), 203-14

67. HD4/26, A Walker, 3 Sept 1677. Wredenhall was also presented, in October 1676, for erecting two new pews in the parish church without licence. Chearme as churchwarden possibly acquiesced in this unauthorised development, and so the presentation may have been at the instigation of Foulkes. Despite this, permission for the pews was granted retrospectively, after mandates were read out in the church during November (*Court Book*, fo. 79v; HRO: AL19/19, *Ms Register of Bishop Croft (1672-82)*, ff. 46r – 47r, 60r, 60v)

68. Both documents are kept at ref. HD4/25

69. HD4/25, Presentment of R Chearme, 29 Aug 1676 (see Appendix, document 2). Chearme subsequently even presented his fellow churchwarden, Joseph Wall, before the Court for refusing to join him in this presentment. Wall had declined to co-operate on the grounds that he would not present Foulkes unless he knew the accusations to be true. Court Book, fo. 80v

70. Testimony of Wall, Garbett, and Coston: HD4/26, Sept 1677

71. ed. A Whiteman, *The Compton Census of 1676: A Critical Edition* (British Academy Records of Social & Economic History, n.s. X), 1986, 255

72. The second and third verses from Comus' song *Your hay it is mow'd*

73. D A Spaeth, *The Church in an Age of Danger: Parsons and Parishioners 1660-1740* (Cambridge, 2000), 141

74. HRO: HD4/4/4, ff.43-4

75. SA, MS 320/6, *Estate Book of Thomas Powys 1665-1670*, 25

76. *Court Book*, fo. 83v

77. HD4/2/16B, W Hopton, 28 Oct 1676

78. HD4/2/16B, M Hopton, 28 Oct 1676

79. HD4/2/16B, G Humphreyes, 30 Oct 1676

80. HD4/25, Article 10, 1 Aug 1676; HD4/2/16B, W Hopton, 28 Oct 1676

81. HD4/26, R Foulkes, 4 Sept 1677, & E Atkinson, 18 Sept 1677

82. Two daughters of William and Katharine Collins were baptized at Stanton Lacy in March 1672 and February 1680, but no children appear between those dates

83. HD4/25, Article 4, 1 Aug 1676. This contemporary euphemism was graphically explored in the song 'The Trooper Watering his Nagg' printed in Henry Playford's *Wit and Mirth: or Pills to Purge Melancholy*, iii (London, 1707), 55, and later reprinted by Thomas D'Urfey in 1719.

84. HD4/26, R Chearme, 10 Mar 1677

85. HD4/2/16B, M Dovey, 28 Oct 1676

86. *Court Book*, fo. 79v

87. *Court Book*, fo. 96r

88. D A Spaeth, 'Common Prayer? Popular observance of the Anglican liturgy in Restoration Wiltshire', in Susan Wright (ed.), *Parish Church & People; Local Studies in Lay Religion 1350-1750* (London, 1988), 127-30; also D A Spaeth, *The Church in an Age of Danger* (Cambridge, 2000), 174-8, 183-4

89. For an exploration of the issues surrounding the courts, moral surveillance, and privacy during the 17th-century, see M Ingram, *Church Courts, Sex and Marriage in England, 1570-1640*, Cambridge 1987 (1990 edn) 242-5

90. HD4/26, W Hopton, 21 Mar 1676/77

91. It was in Francis Underwood's house that Ann was said to have spent about a month while recuperating from her first pregnancy (HD4/2/16B, R Chearme, 30 Oct 1676)

92. HD4/2/16B, J Wood, 30 Oct 1676

93. *Court Book*, fo. 79r

94 HD4/26, E Atkinson, 19 Mar 1676/77

95. HD4/26, J Slade, 26 Feb 1676/77. Slade's predecessor at Bromfield, Henry Maurice, had been of strong puritan leanings, and had resigned the vicarage in 1669. Not long after his testimony, John Slade became rector of Kingsland, in Herefordshire, in August 1678; and subsequently prebendary of Norton in Hereford cathedral in 1684. He died early in 1721

96. HD4/26, W Hopton, 21 Mar 1676/77. The burial of Richard Herbert Esq. was recorded on 25th March 1676, and his coffin was placed in a vault beneath the high altar. It was he who in 1672 had reinstated what is now the chancel of Bromfield parish church, after fire had swept through what was up until then part of his house. See *Shropshire Parish Registers* (Hereford Diocese v – Bromfield), 63; National Library of Wales, Powis Papers, 14226; A L Moir, *Bromfield Priory and Church* (Chester, 1947), 25

97. 'Strong waters' is an archaic term for alcoholic liquor

98. *An Alarme for Sinners,* 7

99. HD4/26, W Bradley, 5 Sept 1677

100. In October 1676, and again in February and September, 1677

101. HD4/26, R Fenton, 1 Sept 1677

102. HD4/26, J Atkinson, 17 Sept 1677. Ann's uncle and godfather, William Whitmore, named in her father's will, had died in June 1668, and his will was proved in the following November (TNA: Prob. 11/328 ff. 288v-290r), and therefore the uncle referred to here must have been his elder brother, Thomas, of Ludstone Hall (1599-1677). Ann was said to have stayed with him after leaving West Felton. It may also be significant that this was within the Royal Peculiar of Bridgnorth and consequently, like West Felton, a place outside the bishop's jurisdiction

103. HD4/26, W Hall, 17 Sept 1677

104. *An Alarme for Sinners,* 11

105. Ref. HD4/25, undated

106. J A Sharpe, *Early Modern England* (2nd edit., 1997), 195

107. HD4/26, Defence Submissions, 4 Sept 1677; J Atkinson, 17 Sept 1677

108. HD4/26, J Atkinson, E Atkinson, 18 Sept 1677

109. HD4/2/16B, W Hopton, 28 Oct 1676

110. Edward Miles junior, carrier, was buried on 25th March 1680. His father was the issuer of at least three varieties of brass halfpenny token during the mid-1660s. See illustration on p.96

111. HD4/26, E Smalman, 24 Sept 1677

112. The Fox Inn stood on the south side of Kiln Lane, now known as Princess Street, on the site later occupied by the Working Mens Hall. It was still one of the largest inns in Shrewsbury in 1838. See L C Lloyd, *The Inns of Shrewsbury* (Shrewsbury, 1942), 27

113. HD4/26, S Wall, 1 Sept 1677

114. The Three Tuns tavern probably stood on a corner site between the Cornmarket and Gullet Shut. It faced the old Market Hall, built in 1595 and still standing today. L C Lloyd, *The Inns of Shrewsbury* (see annotated copy held by Shropshire Archives), 56

115. HD4/26, A Walker, 3 Sept 1677, & E Smalman, 24 Sept 1677

116. HD4/26, R Foulkes, 26 Feb 1677/78

117. HD4/26, 27 Nov 1677

118. See Appendix, document 3

119. HD4/25, E Coats, 18 Mar 1678

120. *Court Book*, fo. 104v

121. *Shropshire Parish Registers* (Hereford Diocese xiv – Ludlow), 502. John Brabant's name also appears among the Ludlow Hearth Tax exemption certificates in 1672. See M A Faraday, 'The Ludlow Poll-Tax Returns of 1667' in *Transactions of the Shropshire Archaeological Society*, LIX (1971/72), 122

122. *Hearth Tax Collectors Book for Worcester 1678-1680*, Worcestershire Historical Society, n.s. vol. 11, 25, 101

123. *Ludlow Parish Register*, 197

124. *Ibid.*, 206

125. *Liber Recordum for 1666-7*, fo. 2r. Worcestershire Record Office, at ref. A 1. box 9

126. *Spetchley Parish Register*; J B Wilson (ed.), *The Parish Book of St. Helen's Church in Worcester*, i (London, 1900), 94-108

127. *Hearth Tax Collectors Book for Worcester 1678-1680*, 49. Brabant was buried at St. Helen's on 14th April, 1682

128. HD4/26, S Brabant, 21 Aug 1678 (see Appendix, document 4)

129. Registrars Files, HD7/20/355 (see Appendix, document 5)

130. HD4/26. Statements of witnesses questioned at West Felton, in the diocese of Lichfield and Coventry, dated 25th September 1678

131. Bodleian Library, MS Tanner 35, fo. 159r

132. *The Execution of Mr. Rob. Foulks, late Minister of Stanton-Lacy in Shropshire*, London: Printed for R.G. 1679, pp. 4; *A true and perfect Relation of the Tryal and Condemnation, Execution and last Speech of that unfortunate Gentleman Mr. Robert Foulks*, London: Printed for L. White in White-cross street, 1679, pp. 8; *The Wonders of Free-Grace: Or, A Compleat History Of all the Remarkable Penitents that have been Executed at Tyburn, and elsewhere for these last Thirty Years*, London, Printed for John Dunton at the Raven in the Poultry, 1690, pp. 37-52

133. J L Rayner & G T Crook (eds.), *The Complete Newgate Calendar*, i (Navarre Society, London, 1926), 275. Traditional and classical herbal abortifacients might include pennyroyal or rue, and concoctions would be taken either to induce abortion, or on the pretext of helping to bring on a period. Nicholas Culpeper's *Complete Herbal* of 1653 warned that a decoction of Ground Pine was 'utterly forbidden for women with child, for it will cause abortion or delivery before the time'.

134. Foulkes maintained that this was so, and there seems little reason to doubt him

135. *An Alarme for Sinners*, 20; *The Wonders of Free-Grace*, 42

136. London Metropolitan Archives: ref. MJ/SR/1556

137. *An Alarme for Sinners*, 21. Thomas Wright, in his *Ludlow Sketches* (Ludlow, 1867), rather harshly considered this declaration 'an unmanly defence, and it would have been better for his memory had it never been written.'

138. Bodleian Library, MS Tanner 35, ff. 159r – 159v

139. *The Wonders of Free Grace*, 42

140. *A true and perfect Relation*, 5

141. Bodleian Library, MS Tanner 35, fo. 159r

142. *A true and perfect Relation*, 5

143. *The Wonders of Free Grace*, 41. William Lloyd also writes of 'the body being found by God's wonderfull Providence'

144. MS Tanner 35, fo. 159v

145. *An Alarme for Sinners*, 20. Samuel Smith (1620-1698) was at that time the Ordinary or prison chaplain at Newgate, among whose functions was to preach to the prisoners and record their confessions. The publication of the latter were one of the perquisites of the post and greatly to his profit, although not in Foulkes' case

146. Ibid., 21. The allegation that Foulkes could argue polygamy, not proscribed in the bible, might be lawful, appears to have been another ruse to discredit him by suggesting that he held unorthodox views, and it has Anabaptist echoes. William Hopton also tried to claim that Foulkes had offered to save Katharine Collins' soul for twopence if she yielded to his advances. Despite all this, there is no evidence whatsoever that he held anything but orthodox beliefs

147. See J L Rayner & G T Crook (eds.), *The Complete Newgate Calendar*, i (Navarre Society, London, 1926), 274-5

148. Lloyd and Burnet were evidently at this time closely associated, appearing in other contexts such as in John Evelyn's diary in July 1679, after interviewing the child prodigy William Wotton. Lloyd was later to be one of the seven bishops imprisoned in the Tower during the reign of James II, for refusing to order the reading of the declaration of indulgence to Catholics from parish pulpits. Following a trial, the seven were acquitted amidst great public rejoicing

149. *An Alarme for Sinners*, London, Printed for Langley Curtis, on Ludgate-Hill, 1679, pp.39

150. Goldie, M. ed., *The Entring Book of Roger Morrice*, ii (Boydell, London, 2007), 92, 103

151. There are at least four variations of the title page, the earliest referring to the date of licensing and stating that the text came 'With an Account of his LIFE' (see p.115). This last was an overstatement, and the words were removed from later versions. The Licensing Act of 1662 expired in the Spring of 1679, and so copies printed after the

Act had lapsed dropped any reference to it. The title page also refers to the text being sent by Foulkes 'at his Death to Doctor Lloyd, Dean of Bangor'. This later became '... William Lloyd, D.D., Dean of Bangor'; and Lloyd was not enthroned as Bishop of St. Asaph until October 1680. A marginal reference on p. 35 to Dr. Simon Patrick's *Devout Christian*, also appears only in earlier copies. The pamphlet was still available from the publisher in the summer of 1682, then still being regularly advertised by Langley Curtis in *The True Protestant Mercury* (see number 169, 16 August 1682)

152. *A true and perfect Relation*, 7

153. *The Wonders of Free-Grace: Or, A Compleat History Of all the Remarkable Penitents that have been Executed at Tyburn, and elsewhere for these last Thirty Years*, London. Printed for John Dunton at the Raven in the Poultry, 1690, 38

154. Andrew Clark, *The Life and Times of Anthony à Wood*, ii (Oxford, 1892), 435; or see OUP abridged edit. (1961), 233-4

155. The full text of his final speech is printed as Appendix, document 6

156. I am indebted to The Venerable Dr W M Jacob, Rector of St.Giles-in-the-Fields, for this information

157. Samuel Newborough was probably the elder brother of John Newborough, headmaster of Eton between 1689 and 1712

158. Her kinship with Lord Craven doubtless played a part in this

159. Bodleian Library, MS Tanner 35, ff. 159r-159v (see Appendix, document 10)

160. MS Tanner 35, fo. 171r (see Appendix, document 11). Lloyd refers to Foulkes' execution (31 Jan 1679) as having taken place 'neer 3 years ago', but there is some doubt whether, in dating his letters simply to January 1682, he was using old or new style dating. The two letters have been bound in date order with others clearly marked 1682/83, and so it is assumed that Ann's return took place in 1682, because of Elizabeth's illness, and not during the summer of 1681

161 *ODNB* (2004), x, 553; HRO: HD4/2/1 and HD4/2/2

162. HRO: AA20 106/2/18 (see Appendix, document 9). Caudle was a sweet spiced drink, of oatmeal gruel flavoured with wine or ale, and taken hot. The silver cup would have had two handles

163. Will of Francis Atkinson, HRO: AA20 106/2/20. He was buried on the same day that he signed his will, the 21st of January

164. HRO: AA20, box 122

165. TNA: Prob. 11/352, fo. 323r; *Hearth Tax Collectors Book for Worcester 1678-1680*, Worcestershire Historical Society, n.s. 11, 106. Joan Foulkes had occupied a nearby property with three hearths

166. *An Alarme for Sinners*, 28-9. What happened to Foulkes' children is at present unknown. A Samuel Foulkes was the father of two children, William and Isabella, baptized in St. Giles without Cripplegate, London, in 1707 and 1709

167. Mary Colbatch, Isabella's younger sister, had married a John Senex, and gave birth to a son, also John, in Ludlow in about November 1678. The boy was destined to become a leading London cartographer and globe maker, and was elected a Fellow of the Royal Society in 1728. Robert Foulkes was, therefore, his uncle, and was executed when Senex was but a few months old

168. P Ripley, 'A Seventeenth-Century Consistory Court Case' in *Bristol and Gloucestershire Archaeological Society Transactions*, C (1982), 211-20

169. Although Littleton complained bitterly that he had been treated unjustly, Bishop Frampton's opinion of his character had not changed by 1688, and this was robustly communicated to the Archbishop of Canterbury. Bodleian Library, MS Tanner 47, ff. 184, 185, 232

170. *Athenian Mercury*, Volume 4, No.16. (21 Nov 1691)

171. Bodleian Library, Vet. A3 e.237 (50)

172. *The Missionary Magazine*, IX (Edinburgh, 1804), 97-244. Practically three-quarters of the original text was reprinted here

173. TNA Prob. 11/354, ff. 198r-200r

174. *Shropshire Parish Registers* (Hereford Diocese x – Claverley), 130; TNA: Prob. 11/328, ff. 288v-290r

175. J Kenyon, *The Popish Plot* (London 1972, repr. 2000), 164

Postscript

VERBAL ARCHAEOLOGY *or* A WIFE'S LAMENT

If you have read this far you will by now have quite an insight into seventeenth century attitudes. You will know that people of all classes were easily drawn into moral temptation and were often obsessed with gossip and intrigue, that suing your neighbours and testifying in court was a major pastime for those who could afford it, and that society was driven by money and morals with sometimes brutal consequences. The dust-dry records of court and church proceedings only hint at the lively, humorous and often sensational stories under the surface that are equally relevant to today's liberal society. Fortunately however these have been preserved for us to rediscover.

Researching this story has resembled an archaeological investigation lasting many years. Stories decay over time like any other artefact, and once the details have been forgotten they start to change and degrade. Occasionally they resurface in altered or unexpected form but it is only with painstaking patience that the full picture can be reconstructed like some ancient pot or structure. As with all archaeology there must inevitably be some speculation, but Peter's informed careful and sensitive reasoning has rewarded us with this fascinating and vivid tale.

Walking the streets of Ludlow or the lanes around Stanton Lacy, visiting Croft Castle, going to Shrewsbury or even Wales, Oxford and London, the long-dead characters from this book seem to press very close. Many years have been spent piecing their very real lives together, with varying success – sometimes there just isn't the evidence. And the gaps are just as interesting – what happened to William Hopton and Mary (and Lord Craven's money), and where did Isabella and the children go after leaving Stanton Lacy? What effect did their father's execution have on them? – did they survive to marry and thrive and lead normal lives? Did Ann find a husband? Did she manage to maintain her dignity and privileged position in society or did she get her comeuppance in the end? Did the people of Stanton Lacy settle down after Foulkes's demise or did they find some other scandal to work upon in the church and alehouse? Ann in particular comes across very clearly as being an attractive, lively, demanding and clever young woman, akin to Thackeray's Becky Sharpe from *Vanity Fair,* and we can't help admiring her, but was this a true picture or has our perception been coloured by the subjective accounts and testimonies? She obviously had status, and the ability to charm and influence the men in her life, but she may have been misrepresented, in particular Foulkes's assertion from the condemned cell that she had instigated her child's murder could have been exaggerated. Where and when did these people die, and in what circumstances?

These questions will probably never be answered, and readers will have to make up their own minds but they will do so in the knowledge that many long hours have been spent searching archives and indexes, transcribing documents, pondering over the minutiae, trekking to distant record offices and churches, taking photographs, missing meals working late at night at the expense of sleep, poring over maps and drawings and writing and rewriting text.

It has been a fascinating and enriching detective story experience, and we hope that you have enjoyed journeying with us despite the bitter and tragic end to the story.

Debby Klein

ACKNOWLEDGEMENTS

There are many to whom I am greatly indebted for helping, both directly and indirectly, in the preparation of this book. I would like to thank the staff of the Bodleian Library, Oxford; the Corporation of London Guildhall Library; the Herefordshire Record Office; the London Metropolitan Archives; the Shropshire Archives; and the Worcestershire Record Office, who have all helped in making research material available.

I would particularly like to thank Andy Johnson, who kindly read a very imperfect early draft of the text, and gave me valuable advice. Also the Venerable Archdeacon Dr. W M Jacob, rector of St. Giles-in-the-Fields, who kindly supplied information about Foulkes' burial; Ivor Lewis, churchwarden of St. Tydecho's parish church at Mallwyd; and also Christopher Potter, for calling my attention to an important deposition in which Foulkes revealed his place of birth. I stand greatly indebted to the late David Lloyd MBE for reading the text; and also my special thanks to Jean Heaven, both for reading an early draft, and for our discussions that gave me the benefit of her considerable knowledge of and insights into the human condition. My publishers, Merlin Unwin and Karen McCall, have been unfailingly enthusiastic and supportive throughout the preparation of this book, and both their suggestions and our fruitful collaboration have made its birth a much less daunting process than I had anticipated.

I would above all like to thank my wife Debby, who has contributed both the delightful maps, illustrations and a Postscript; and without whose sense of literary style this book would have been very much the poorer. Not only have our lengthy discussions always been stimulating, but she has also had to put up with the usual isolation of being an author's wife!

This book is the result of a long process of gestation, although for the most part the work of the last two years. Very shortly before the finalised text of the first edition was delivered to the publishers, a long-awaited new edition of the *Oxford Dictionary of National Biography* was launched in 2004, in which a new and substantially longer entry concerning the life and career of Robert Foulkes now appeared.

Such a work as the *Dictionary* will have undoubted authority, but readers of both accounts may become aware of a few discrepancies in assertions of fact. Amongst these is the statement that Foulkes murdered his illegitimate child in London in November 1678 by strangling it, an assertion derived from two slim contemporary printed pamphlets. This curiously flies in the face of two important primary manuscript sources, both cited by the author in his own notes, which confirm that Foulkes cut the child's throat with a knife on the 11th of December! There are other differences, but these have also been carefully checked against the sources, and my original text remains substantially unaltered. I should add that the online edition of the *Oxford Dictionary* has since been amended.

It only remains for me to add that I would be extremely grateful for any additional information that readers may have concerning people, places, or events mentioned in this book. I would be particularly interested to know of any living descendants of the Atkinson or Foulkes families.

Peter Klein

INDEX

ALSO PUBLISHED BY MERLIN UNWIN BOOKS
see details: www.merlinunwin.co.uk

The Yellow Earl Douglas Sutherland

A Shropshire Lad A.E. Housman

Nearest Earthly Place to Paradise:
          the literary landscape of Shropshire

It Happened in Shropshire Bob Burrows

It Happened in Gloucestershire Phyllida Barstow

It Happened in Lancashire Malcolm Greenhalgh

It Happened in Lincolnshire David Clark